Christmas at the Falling Down Guesthouse

Lilly Bartlett

Copyright 2017 ©Michele Gorman
Cover image ©TierneyMJ

All characters and events in this publication, other than those clearly in the public domain, are fictitious and any resemblance to real persons, living or dead, is purely coincidental.

All rights reserved. No part of this publication may be reproduced, stored in a retrieval system, or transmitted, in any form or by any means, without the prior permission of the publisher.

Also by Lilly Bartlett
The Not So Perfect Plan to Save Friendship House
The Big Dreams Beach Hotel
The Big Little Wedding in Carlton Square
The Second Chance Café in Carlton Square

Michele Gorman
Match Me If You Can
The Curvy Girls Club
The Curvy Girls Baby Club
Perfect Girl
Christmas Carol
Life Change
Single in the City (Single in the City 1)
Misfortune Cookie (Single in the City 2)
Twelve Days to Christmas (Single in the City 3)

A note on this edition

This novel was written and edited in British English, including all spelling, grammar, punctuation and figures of speech.

CHAPTER ONE

I know I'm dreaming by the way the gorgeous bloke grasps my hand and gazes into my eyes. A real man hasn't stared at me with such devotion since the time I reprogrammed my friend's husband's PlayStation.

Just as the dreamy bloke leads me from the pub table into his bedroom next door – what the hell, it's my dream, right? – and I start wondering if I've dream-shaved my legs, his mobile starts ringing.

'Are you going to get that?'

'Get what?' he murmurs into my neck as pieces of clothing fall to the floor. 'I don't hear anything.'

'Your phone is ringing.'

Aggravation starts nibbling at my ardour as his flippin' phone keeps at it.

'I don't hear it.'

'Oh, for God's sake, it's right there on the table!' I can't even get any peace and quiet in my own imagination. Angrily, I reach for his phone.

But there is no dreamy bloke and his phone isn't ringing.

My landline is.

Blearily, I glance at the bedside alarm clock. 1.36am. It's the hour of emergencies and booty calls. But my booty hadn't been called since Tony Blair was Prime Minister. So it must be panic, not passion that's quickening my pulse.

'Hello?' My voice comes out porridge-thick.

'Is this Lottie Crisp?'

'Yes.' The panic blooms in my chest. Mabel. Is it Mabel? No. She's sound asleep in the other room. At least I hope she is.

'This is Doctor Lonergan at Glan Clwyd hospital in Bodelwyddan.'

I sprint with the phone to my daughter's door and push it open. Her little body hardly makes a bump under her Spiderman duvet. One socked foot sticks out bravely over the edge. Mabel's not afraid of monsters, under her bed or anywhere else. I could learn a thing or two from my seven-year-old.

Of course I want to pounce on her and hug her till my heart stops thumping. But sleeping dogs and children should never be disturbed.

'I'm afraid there's been an accident involving your Aunt Kate,' Dr Lonergan is saying. 'Her car went off the road the day before yesterday. We've been trying to reach her family and just now got your details.'

'I'm her only family.' The rushing in my ears is drowning out the doctor's voice. 'Is she... dead?'

'No, she's alive, but she's in Critical Care. Can you

come?'

'Not until morning. The next train to Wales won't be until morning.'

'Come as soon as you can,' she says. 'We've induced a coma to help her body recover.'

I can't believe this is happening again.

Aunt Kate is the liveliest person I've ever known. Though I'd have said that about my parents too, and look how they ended up.

It's still dark when I creep into Mabel's room early the next morning.

She's going to hate me for this. 'Sugarpea?' I rub her duvet-warm back and listen for her breathing to change. 'Mabel? Wake up.'

She inhales one long breath. 'Not yet, Mummy.'

'I'm sorry, but we have to get up extra-early this morning. We get to go to Wales today.'

I'm trying to make this sound like a great adventure instead of a panicky dash to my auntie's bedside.

At least Celine packed Mabel's bag before she flew to the Philippines for her own Christmas holiday. She knows I'd probably have brought Mabel to Wales with fifteen jumpers, her favourite blue tutu and no socks.

'But we're not leaving for two days,' says Mabel, rubbing her eyes with the back of her hand.

'We've got to go early.'

She sits up. 'I can't, Mummy. I have other plans.'

'I know Theresa's birthday is tomorrow.' She's been looking forward to her best friend's party for nearly a month. 'But this is important. You can still ring her to wish her happy birthday.'

My daughter's jaw sets. Whenever she does that, I see her father.

That's the only time I ever see him.

'Please, Mabel, don't make this difficult. Now get up and clean your teeth. We've got to leave in twenty minutes to make our train.'

'I'm not going!' She throws the duvet over her head. 'I told you, I have other plans.'

'And I told you that you are going, young lady. So please get up and clean your teeth. I'll pack us some breakfast for the train. Come on. Now!'

'You're a terrible Mummy!' she cries. 'And I hope that one day a big hairy monster comes and flushes you down the loo.'

Don't you dare smile, Lottie Crisp. Everyone knows that's the first lesson in child-rearing. I just wish I knew what lesson numbers two through infinity were.

'Well, until that monster gets here, I'm afraid you're stuck with me. Sorry about that.' Gently, I pull the duvet down and kiss her soft blonde hair. 'Teeth cleaned please, and I'll explain everything when we're on the train.'

I need a bit of time to think. There must be a good way to admit that what I promised her three years ago might be a lie.

We board the train at Euston Station with just a few other sleep-deprived passengers. It's still four days before Christmas and most people will have to work tomorrow to wrap up before they go off for the holidays.

Which I should be doing too. My boss won't be thrilled that I've had to leave early. It's no use playing on his sympathy either. Real, live feelings give him a rash. He's a software developer like me, and loves his binary code, also like me. I didn't have time to write a programme that said Sorry-I'm-leaving-my-project-unfinished-but-I'm-terrified-my-auntie-will-die-and-my-family-is-more-important-than-the-latest-war-game-for-children. Maybe animated with a dancing paperclip.

Mabel is a little less grumpy by the time we find our seats on the train. 'I can't wait to see Aunt Kate!' she says. 'Do you think she'll have Welsh cakes for us when we arrive? I could just *murder* a Welsh cake.'

That child sponges up everything I say. I really do have to watch myself.

'We're going early because we need to see Aunt Kate in the hospital,' I tell her.

'Is she there getting her nose refreshed?'

When I went for moral support to my friend's nose job surgery last year, I told Mabel she was going in to freshen up her nose.

'No, Aunt Kate's nose is just fine the way it is.' I hope that's still true. 'She's in the hospital because she's had an accident.'

'Well, she shouldn't be in that big house all by herself. She's not young anymore.'

I cringe at my words parroted back at me. I *really* have to watch what I say. 'It wasn't in the house, honey. It was a car accident.'

Her eyes widen. 'Like Granny and Grandad?' she whispers. 'You said it wouldn't happen again.'

'No, no! Not like them. The doctor said that Aunt Kate is still—' Alive, I almost say. 'She's in the hospital and the doctors are doing everything they can to make her better so that she can spend Christmas with us.'

Mabel slumps against me. 'I was scared. I'm glad she's all right.'

Then she straightens up. 'Can I give her my Christmas present early? That might cheer her up.'

Finally, my tears come. I look out the window so Mabel won't see them. I'm not sure I can go through all this again.

It had been early morning here when the doctor rang from the A&E in Australia, but he hadn't had to search for my contact details that time. Mum and Dad had everything neatly written in a small notebook in Mum's handbag. They were careful people like that.

'Is this Lottie Crisp?'

As soon as I heard the man's bouncy Aussie accent, I knew something was wrong.

My parents had dreamed for years about spending a month travelling around Australia. Finally, for Dad's sixtieth birthday, they were doing it. I knew their itinerary off by heart. A week in Sydney, then a flight to Melbourne where they'd visit some friends, then a two-week drive through the outback.

'Miss Crisp,' said the man as I braced myself. His laid-back accent didn't fool me. 'There's been an accident involving your parents. I'm terribly sorry.'

I only half-heard the rest of what he said. The outback, drunk driver, Mum killed instantly. Dad fought to stay alive but his injuries were too severe. Could I come?

I had to bring their bodies back to England. That was the worst part of the first few days, sitting on that plane knowing my parents were lying in the hold with all the holidaymakers' luggage.

Aunt Kate came to stay with Mabel so that I could go. We'd only had a few hours together before I had to leave for the airport. Even though it was her only brother who'd died, and her beloved sister-in-law, she was as rock-solid as the Welsh cakes she made for Mabel's tea.

'I would do anything to take this pain away, my sweet Lottie, anything,' she said as she smothered me in her ample bosom with the grip of a Sumo wrestler. 'I'm here for you, do you understand? Whatever you need, I'm here for you, my darling girl. We'll get through this together, you, me and Mabel.'

We did get through it, together, though I've had more than a few harsh words since then for whoever decides our fates.

If they now think they're going to take my Aunt Kate too, they've got another thing coming. We Crisps don't go down without a struggle.

CHAPTER TWO

The train ride to Rhyl is smooth, but my mind skitters from one horrific scenario to another. What will I find when we get to the hospital? If only I could rewind the past seventy-two hours and keep Aunt Kate safely off the road. She's got the eyesight of a mole. She should never have been driving anyway. If everything had gone to plan, Mabel and I would be turning up in two days' time, full of excitement for our first Welsh countryside Christmas with Aunt Kate at her countryside B&B.

    She's run the business since before Mabel was born, but always shuts up between Christmas and New Year's so she can come stay with us in London.

    This year though, Aunt Kate is taking in paying guests for the holidays. It's the last thing she wants to do – and it's always hard to pin Aunt Kate down on details – but something about her bank loan being dependent on the B&B getting a certain rating by the end of the year means that she has to host the reviewer over Christmas. So Mabel and I said we'd bring the Crisp family Christmas to her instead.

That was the idea anyway.

We're the only passengers to exit the two-carriage train in Rhyl. From what Aunt Kate has said, it's a typical Victorian resort town. It's about as far out of season as you can get now, but in summer the beachfront probably bustles with swim-suited families, all burnt to a crisp and ready to eat their own weight in Welsh rock and candyfloss.

That sounds like heaven right now.

I tuck Mabel's scarf into her collar against the slanting rain, and pull my coat more tightly around me.

'Aunt Kate lives here?' she asks, peering at the ornate ironwork on the station, with its paintwork tattooed with rust from the sea air, and its glass roof.

'No, not in town. I think she's about fifteen miles from here in an area called Snowdonia.'

'Will there be snow there?'

'It feels cold enough, doesn't it? But I don't think so. Not where the B&B is anyway. Maybe up in the mountains.'

'Are we going there now?'

'Not yet. We need to go see her at the hospital first, remember?'

A lone taxi sits at the front of the station.

The driver gets out to load our bags into the boot, hugging his huge sheepskin coat more tightly around his tall frame. He's dishevelled in a way that would make him a hipster in London, but something about his stained jeans and ancient boots tells me that his stubble and too-long dark hair aren't fashion statements.

I'm one to talk. If not for the doctor's early morning call, I'd be getting a haircut and colour at lunchtime today. Wales is just going have to deal with my dark roots…. and wayward brows and chipped nails. Aunt Kate's never really cared about how I look anyway. She always thinks I'm beautiful. Which is a bit of a stretch.

Mabel is, however, beautiful. She's got the same pale blonde, straight hair that I had at her age, which I now have to pay £80 quid for. But her eyes are chocolate-dark like her father's instead of my nothingy-hazel. And she's already long-limbed and graceful, so she also missed out on the Crisp family short-arseness.

My gorgeous girl.

'We're going to Glan Clwyd hospital, please,' I tell the driver.

He pulls out from the station like he's fleeing the scene. We hurtle up the quiet road and careen around the corner.

'You can slow down a little. It's not an emergency. Mabel, check your seatbelt. You're sure it's on?'

His motoring skills don't improve as we race along the rural two-lane road, sandwiched between the sea and sheep-filled fields. If this is how people drive around here, then I'm not surprised Aunt Kate crashed her car.

My heart starts racing when the hospital comes

into view. What if we get to the desk and the nurse looks at us with pity as she works out how to tell us that we're too late?

No, I won't think like that. For Mabel's sake, I've got to stay positive.

'We're here to see Kate Crisp, please,' I tell the plump, pleasant-looking woman behind the reception desk. 'She's in Critical Care.'

She taps her keyboard. 'Just down that corridor, love. Now what you do is go through the double doors on your left. The nurse inside can take you straight to her.'

'Oh, okay, that's brilliant, thank you!' I find myself smiling. She's the perfect hospital front desk person, with the type of positive bedside manner that could make you look forward to having your leg amputated.

When we get to the Critical Care desk, the young nurse says, 'You're looking for Ms Crisp? She's right this way.' As if we're just meeting her for lunch.

We follow her down another short corridor.

'Please clean your hands whenever you go into the room.'

I gesture for Mabel to hold her palms under the liquid disinfectant.

'It stinks.'

'I know it does, but it kills the germs.'

'Does it smother them?'

'Something like that.'

Aunt Kate has the room to herself. She's in the bed closest to the door, with a mask over her face and tubes running from her arms.

'Is she dead?' Mabel whispers.

I shake my head, not trusting my voice. Her face is swollen and her forehead has turned a nasty shade of purple. There's a stitched-up laceration over her eye. 'She's just sleeping.'

'I'll see if the doctor is free,' the nurse says, hurrying out.

I go to my aunt and gently touch her hand. 'I'm here, Aunt Kate. Mabel and I are here.'

'Can she hear you?'

'I'm not sure, but I think so. Do you want to talk to her? I'm sure she'd love that.'

She nods and shuffles very close to the bed.

'Hi Aunt Kate, it's me, Mabel. You'll probably know it's me even with your eyes closed because of my voice. We had a nice journey on the train. We had regular seats, but then because there weren't many people on, we moved to a table. Mummy said it was better for her computer, but then she forgot her computer and she swore. Not the F word, though, just the S word. I still told her that ladies don't swear. That's right, isn't it, Mummy?'

'That's right, I shouldn't have said that.'

An older woman joins us as Mabel continues talking to Aunt Kate as though they're chatting over tea and cake.

Dr Lonergan smiles as she introduces herself. She's got a kind but serious face. It's a trustworthy face. She takes Aunt Kate's chart from the end of the bed and then gestures outside.

'I'll just be out here, Mabel. I bet Aunt Kate would

love to hear about your Christmas pageant.'

'She's in a coma?' I ask Dr Lonergan under the bright corridor lights.

'Yes, a medically-induced coma. There's a lot of swelling around her brain, so we want to help it heal by eliminating any non-essential functions.'

'Then it's not the kind where you don't know if she's going to wake up?'

Dr Lonergan shakes her head. 'We've administered drugs to induce it, so once we remove the drugs, she'll wake up.'

'When will you do that?'

'Not until the swelling has gone down in her brain. There may not be brain damage, but we won't know for sure until the swelling subsides. That could take a few days or a few weeks. We're monitoring her closely and, as you can see, she's on a respirator to help her breathe.'

'She's going to be okay then?'

'She was very lucky she was wearing her seatbelt. As was the other passenger. But the other car impacted on your Aunt's side, which is why she sustained more serious injuries. She's also got a broken tibia – her leg – which we've set. That should heal within six to eight weeks and then she can have the cast removed. Do you have any other questions?'

'No. Yes. You said there was a passenger? Who was it?'

She glances at her paperwork. 'A Ms Evans was also involved in the accident.'

Ms Evans? I think she's Aunt Kate's cook, though

she usually called her by her job description. 'And she's all right?'

'She fractured her arm but she was treated and discharged. I believe she's staying with her niece over in Dyserth. Do you know it?'

'No, I'm not from around here.' Like that isn't obvious from my London accent. 'Do you have her phone number?'

'I'll have the nurse get it for you when you leave. The visiting hours in Critical Care are from four o'clock till seven each evening. You can stay today because you've just arrived and there isn't another patient in your aunt's room. Will you be coming back tomorrow?'

Yes, I tell her, and every day until Aunt Kate is well again. There's no way I'll leave her. Mabel and I will be spending Christmas in Wales.

'Please leave your contact details with reception,' says Dr Lonergan. 'And will you be staying at her house?'

'Yes. We'll be there if you need us. Oh. I haven't got keys.'

'Everything she had in the car is in the cabinet by her bed. If her keys are there, feel free to take them with you.'

'Thank you. Can I go back in to her now?'

'Of course. I'm sorry this happened so close to Christmas,' she says. 'It probably isn't how you thought you'd be spending the holiday.'

Definitely not.

Then I remember why Aunt Kate couldn't come to London this year.

The reviewer and his family don't know about the accident. They'll still turn up on the 24th expecting a Christmas holiday.

I lean down to kiss Aunt Kate's cool cheek.

'You don't have to worry about anything, Aunt Kate, just concentrate on getting well. I'll take good care of the B&B until you're fit again, I promise.'

When the reception nurse gives me the phone number where Cook is staying, I ring it straightaway. I'm definitely going to need her help over the coming week.

'Hello, is that Ms Evans? The cook at Kate Crisp's B&B?'

'No, it's her niece Bronwyn. Who's this?'

I remember that Bronwyn is Aunt Kate's cleaner. Perfect. I'll need her help too. She listens as I explain who I am.

'What do you want?'

She sounds angry. Surely she's not blaming me or Aunt Kate for what happened?

'Well, I wondered when your aunt will be able to come back to work.'

'Probably in the new year,' she says.

'The new year! But we need her now. I understand that she's recovering from the accident, and maybe she can't cook easily with a broken arm, but I was hoping...'

'It's impossible. We're leaving tomorrow morning,' she says. 'We're going to Spain to recuperate.'

'What, both of you? But you weren't even in the

accident. Aren't you coming to work either?'

'No, as I said, we're going to Spain. You can't expect me to send my poorly auntie on her own.'

'But who's going to clean the B&B while you're gone?'

'I didn't know I'd be needed, did I? With Kate in hospital, I didn't think there'd be any work for me anyway. I've got to go. Auntie is waiting for her lunch.'

'Wait, please, wait,' you skiving little cow, I don't say. 'If your aunt can't come to work, could she at least tell me what I need to know about the place? I've never even been there.'

'She's not up to talking right now.'

'Couldn't she, I don't know, email me with some instructions? Here's my email address.'

I'm not convinced she's writing anything down.

'Please, Bronwyn. I have no idea what I'm doing. Can you please ask her to at least do that before you leave?'

She sighs. 'I'll ask her, but we're very busy. We have to pack and EasyJet charges a fortune for checked bags. I don't know how we're going to get everything into carry-ons.'

Ooh, boo hoo, poor Bronwyn and Cook, having to worry about how to pack for their holiday in the sun.

It's still raining when we leave the hospital. I should have asked reception to call us a taxi.

'Here, button up, Mabel, so you don't catch a cold.'

A car pulls up and the door opens.

'You again?' I say to the taxi driver who dropped us off.

'I waited.'

'We went in over an hour ago. You didn't need to wait.'

'You're probably my only fare for the day,' he says. 'Are you going back to the train station?'

'No, to my Aunt's B&B.'

I read him the address from the letter Aunt Kate sent with directions for our arrival.

Again, he corrects my pronunciation.

'Mummy, we're staying at Aunt Kate's when she's not there?'

'Yes, because we'll want to see her every day until she's well, won't we? And we can make the house look lovely for when she comes home.'

We've got no choice. In three days, Aunt Kate's hotel will be full of guests. Someone's got to be there to welcome them or she might not have a business to come home to.

Granted, I'm not the most domesticated person. But I'll do my best. The B&B should impress the reviewer on looks alone. I've never actually seen it in person, but I know it's gorgeous. Thanks to Aunt Kate's descriptions over the years, I can picture it as clearly as if I lived there. It'll be the perfect backdrop for Christmas, with its grand two story Victorian façade, formal parlour and library, large hall and dining room. There'll be cosy evenings playing board games in front of the roaring fire or snuggled up with a book on one of the embroidered sofas. Even if it doesn't stop raining, the guests can at least get some daylight in the conservatory that looks out to the hills.

It sounds like heaven. The rating should only be a formality, really. It's just a shame it's got to happen now. Even if I could convince the guests to cancel their Christmas, I haven't got the faintest idea how to get in touch with them.

Like it or not, I'm about to become a B&B hostess.

CHAPTER THREE

'Can you please slow down?' I ask the taxi driver again. He doesn't seem to know where his brake pedal is and he keeps swerving over the centre line. But after thirty fraught minutes, we're finally turning into a steep drive.

'Are you sure this is the address?' I ask. 'It doesn't look right.'

The winter-bare trees have dropped many of their branches, which the taxi's wheels crunch over as we pull into the circular drive. And the house is, well...

He takes Aunt Kate's letter from me again.

'Yes, this is it. I'll get your bags.'

I'd get out and help him, but I'm rooted to the back seat.

This house is completely derelict. The once-white stucco and mock-Tudor façade is streaked and stained with neglect. The elements have bowed and bloated the window sills.

One corner of the steeply gabled roof is tile-free.

The wooden joists poke out like badly broken bones.

I just can't reconcile what I'm seeing with Aunt Kate's descriptions of her dreamy gingerbread house in the woods. This isn't a dream house. It's a nightmare.

The enormity of what I've promised Aunt Kate is starting to sink in. That reviewer and his whole family will arrive, *to this*, in less than seventy-two hours.

'Mummy, is it haunted?' She grabs my hand.

'I'm sure it's not haunted, sugarpea. After all, it's Aunt Kate's home.'

How could I have let my aunt live here for all these years? I should have come up long before this.

'Then why are you crying?'

'Oh, I'm being silly. It's just that there's a lot to do before Aunt Kate's guests arrive.'

The driver opens my door. 'Is everything all right?'

He has a kind face and his deep brown eyes are full of concern. Or maybe he's just afraid I can't pay his fare.

My legs are shaking as I stand up. 'Not really, no. In fact, it's about as far from all right as I can imagine. We've got guests coming for Christmas in three days and the cook and housekeeper are buggering off to Spain. I'm all alone here.'

'Oh, well,' he says, 'Bronwyn has always wanted to go to the Costa del Sol.'

'Well, I'm really glad she'll finally get to work on her tan, but where does that leave me? I can't run this whole place by myself. I have no idea what I'm doing. And look at it.'

Tears fill my eyes again. It's hopeless. I can't even cook, let alone rebuild a roof.

'I wish I could help you.'

He actually looks like he means that. 'Can you cook?' I ask in sudden desperation.

His expression turns from pity to suspicion. 'Why?'

'Because if you can, I'll pay you £1,000 cash to help me for the next few days. Until the 26th when the guests leave.'

'Well I can't really-'

'Please! I don't know what else to do. My aunt is in a coma. That's why we were at the hospital. And it's too late now to cancel the guests' stay.' It all tumbles out. 'It's a reviewer and his family. Aunt Kate scheduled them because she needs a star rating or the bank is going to make her sell the B&B. This is her whole life. Do you know my aunt?'

He shakes his head, rubbing the dark stubble that peppers his chin. 'I only know Bronwyn because we were at school together. A thousand quid you said? Cash?'

That was meant to be for our week's holiday in the spring. 'Yes, and I'll even give you half today and half on the 26th. I'd need you to cook and help me get the place fixed up before they come. Well, basically I'll need you to do whatever you can to help. Is it a deal?'

I pray he'll say yes. Otherwise Mabel is going to have to learn some carpentry skills pretty sharpish.

He puts his hand out and envelops mine in its warmth. 'Deal. I'll drive you to the cash machine back in

Rhyl. I'm Danny. What's your name?'

'Lottie, and this is Mabel. Nice to meet you.'

I just hope he's more domestic than I am.

Try not to judge me when I tell you this, but I've only lived away from my parents for a few years in my entire life. That was when I went to university. It makes me sound really sheltered, doesn't it? But what happened was that I fell in love with Mabel's father in my final year. And then I fell pregnant. And he got scared.

But as soon as I saw those two pink lines on the wee stick, I knew that I wanted the little person growing inside me, and that my parents would be supportive. I never imagined just how supportive they'd turn out to be.

I waddled through my classes, morning-, noon- and night-sick, but so excited to meet my child at the end of it all. She came into the world with a full head of hair and a strong set of lungs and we've been a family of two ever since.

I moved back to my parents' Hampstead house where my old room was waiting for me. Mum painted the spare room lilac and stencilled fairies all over the walls for her granddaughter.

By then, Celine had been part of our family for nearly my whole life. We didn't have that much extra money when I was growing up, but with both Mum and Dad working at the university, they needed someone to look after the house and, sometimes, me. Celine started as a one-day-a-week cleaner, but she always found time to cook delicious dinners on the days she came. Eventually the whole family was addicted to her Filipino dishes and she took on more days as the years went by.

Then, when I was around ten, Celine's landlord turned nasty. He threatened to double her rent and report her to Immigration if she didn't pay up. But Celine's work status here was perfectly legal, so she told him to get stuffed. That was when Mum and Dad invited her to live with us so that she wouldn't have to deal with any more dodgy landlords. As long as the house in Hampstead is in our family, Celine has a home.

With such a fantastic cook around, it's no wonder that I never really learned my way around the kitchen. Things might have been different if I'd lived with Mabel's father, but that was never going to happen.

Danny drives us back at the B&B, me with a lighter bank account and Danny with a grin on his face.

The B&B hasn't improved while we were away. If anything, it looks even more dire.

'Time to go inside,' I say to Mabel, taking her hand. A tiny part of me hopes that we'll be surprised. Maybe Aunt Kate kept up the inside where her guests spent the most time. Then who'd care if the outside was a bit shabby?

I can imagine her draping the rooms in sumptuous velvets and brocades. Once an opera singer, she's always had an eye for the dramatic. She used to drag me along Notting Hill's Portobello Road and to

Grays Antique Centre nearly every weekend that she visited. We searched for brocade footstools and gilded mirrors and chairs or tables with elegant legs (Aunt Kate has a thing for elegant legs). All those purchases over the years must have found their way into the B&B.

By the time I wriggle the key in the lock just the right way to open the large wooden front door, I'm nearly sure it'll look like the prop room at the Royal Opera House.

I take about two steps inside the murky hall. 'Oof. Bollocks!'

'Mummy, are you okay?'

I don't know which to rub first, my throbbing toe or my knees where they've hit the floor. 'I'm fine, I just tripped.'

'You said a swear word.'

'Yes, that wasn't very clever of me, was it?'

'I guess your aunt planned some renovations,' Danny says from behind us. When he sheds his giant coat, I can see that he's a bit older than he first seemed. I'm guessing in his early thirties. 'Look at all these tins of paint.'

As I look around, my hopeful bubble bursts. This is definitely no Royal Opera House.

Three tall windows run along one side of the wide entrance, and a staircase climbs up the other side. But the grimy windowpanes let in only weak winter light.

'I guess we may as well try to see what we're dealing with.'

I hoist up the sash panes on every window so the daylight can reach the darkened corners.

'It's yucky,' Mabel says.

It's worse than yucky. The walls are pockmarked with holes and painted a dreary yellowish brown.

'Who'd use that colour in a house?' I ask.

'I think it was probably a different colour to start with,' Danny says. 'It's yellowed over the years.'

It's got the patina of nicotine-stained fingers and the far corner is streaked with water damage. The varnish is worn off the floorboards where feet have trod over the decades, and everything needs a good wash. Whatever Bronwyn does with her time here, clearly it doesn't involve much soap and water.

Slowly we walk through the rest of the house, like timid tomb raiders. Every gasp from Danny or Mabel makes me jump, expecting the worst. It's obvious that the house was grand once upon a time. The parlour is large and overcrowded with Aunt Kate's elegant-legged tables. I run my hand over a little mahogany side table with an unusual marquetry top.

'Mabel, do you remember when we found this, in that skip in Highgate?'

She smiles. 'You climbed in with the rubbish.'

The things I do for my aunt. 'And we brought it home and Grandad fixed the legs?'

Mabel's smile fades. 'Mummy? Will Aunt Kate die like Granny and Grandad did?'

'Ahem, I'll have a look upstairs,' Danny says, considerately making himself scarce.

I lead Mabel to one of the silver and red Chinese silk sofas. At least they're in good shape.

'Honey, the doctor said that Aunt Kate should be

okay when she wakes up. She's only sleeping now so that her body gets the chance to heal itself.'

'So, she definitely won't die?' Mabel's eyes search my face.

I'd love to give her that kind of absolute certainty. Children should have that. But I can't lie to her. 'I don't think she will. I'm not planning on it, that's for sure. Do you still worry about something happening to me?'

When she nods, my heart breaks a little. How am I supposed to make her feel secure? I haven't got the authority to tell the Grim Reaper to bugger off and bother someone else.

I hug her little body to mine. 'Well, I'm not going anywhere, and neither are you. We've got too much living to do!'

She returns my smile.

'Let's go see what the rest of the house looks like, okay?'

'Yes, that's quite enough of this morbid talk for one day,' says my world-weary seven-year-old.

Danny bounds down the stairs just as we're coming out of the dining room. 'How's it looking down here?' he asks.

'I think the ceiling may be coming down in the dining room, and there are mouse droppings in the kitchen sink. I'm afraid to ask what you've found upstairs.'

He shakes his head. 'Mushrooms are literally growing on the floorboards in the bedrooms, and mould up the walls.'

'Mushrooms? I guess that makes them local

produce. Maybe we can cook them for the fry-ups.' When DIY gods give you mushrooms, make omelettes.

As he pretends to think about it, I notice that he's got lovely big hooded eyes. They remind me of those 1930s film stars photos of Marlene Dietrich.

Though nobody would mistake Danny for a woman.

'Hmm, home-grown mushroom poisoning,' he says. 'Maybe not. I think your Aunt was optimistic when she got all that paint. This place needs a lot more than a coat on the walls. It needs a structural engineer. And a roofer.'

'Well, we've only got three days to do what we can and hope the place doesn't fall down before the guests leave. At least the furniture is all right. There's just too much of it. But yes, Aunt Kate is definitely a person who looks on the bright side.'

She and Dad were opposites in a lot of ways. While he did the sensible thing – going to university, studying hard and gaining respectability in professorial circles, his little sister was travelling by campervan across Europe, trying to make a go of her operatic career. Whenever their parents told her she was nuts, she just laughed and hugged them. There wasn't much that Aunt Kate couldn't overcome with a giggle, a hug, a wing and a prayer.

She did gain a bit of success as an opera singer, and got small parts performing around Europe.

She was dreadful with money though. She didn't mind being paid for her roles in clothes instead of cash so, Dad liked to say, her closets filled up instead of her bank account. But that was okay with her. 'My life is rich and full,' she said. 'My purse doesn't need to be.'

CHAPTER FOUR

'What are you doing?' Danny asks the next morning, possibly wondering why I'm standing on the dining room table in my pyjamas holding my phone towards the crumbling ceiling.

'Oh, you're early.' I pull Aunt Kate's velvet robe around me. I'm sure she won't mind me using it when it's cold enough in here to see your breath.

It was nearly midnight by the time he left last night. We'd worked straight through, but when I got up this morning it didn't look like we'd made much difference.

We did find all the sheets and towels at least, and there's plenty of formal china and glassware for the guests. Today's when the heavy work really starts.

'I'm trying to get a signal,' I tell him. 'I'll go outside in a minute, but I wanted to see what the reception was like inside the house. So far it's a black hole.'

The reviewer might not want to stand on the dining table to send a text.

'Mine's dead too,' says Danny, checking his own phone. 'You could try the conservatory.'

Sure enough, my phone whistles with new emails as soon as I reach the ornate glasshouse.

The noise startles one of the pigeons who's been napping on the floor. He takes flight through a broken window while the rest of his cooing friends watch me have a minor heart attack.

'Hey Danny?' I call back inside. 'You're not a pigeon-whisperer, are you? It's an aviary out here. If you can persuade them all to go outside then we can clean the poo off the floor.' And cover that window to lock them out.

It's frigid, but with the wood-burning stove going in the middle of the room, and the addition of some sofas and chairs, it might pass for shabby chic instead of just shabby. At least there's a phone signal.

I scroll through my emails, clicking open the one from my boss. *Just keep me updated*, it reads, *and let me know when you think you'll be back. I hope your aunt is okay.*

Then I see on Bronwyn's email. It's only a few lines long, but at least it's something.

Dear Lottie, we're at the airport and Bronwyn is typing this on her phone. I'm terribly sorry about your aunt and I do hope she'll be well again soon. Our prayers are with her.

Here's what you need to know about the house:

- *Mingus's food is under the sink. He likes fish instead of the chicken but he'll eat whatever you put out when he gets hungry*
- *Always!! wait five minutes to turn on the taps after flushing the loo*
- *There's coal in the cellar for the wood burners*
- *I believe the reviewer is called Rupert Grey-Smythe*
- *We have mice*
- *Watch out for the 8.30 train*
- *Don't forget about the chickens*

Good luck!

Chickens? If we've got chickens then Danny will have a fresh supply of eggs for breakfast. The morning is looking up already.

I leave him in the kitchen to acquaint himself with the appliances while I check on Mabel.

'Mummy?' she calls as soon as I open the door.

'Yes, sweetie. Did you sleep well?'

'I'm still sleepy,' she says. 'But I'm too excited to stay in bed.'

'Maybe a shower will wake you up. Let me just go in first to make sure it's working, okay?' I tuck the thick duvet around her. 'Have another little rest and I'll let you know when it's ready.'

I counted three bathrooms upstairs. That's not bad for seven guest rooms. Considering how old the house is, you wouldn't expect en-suites in every room. Though the reviewer *can* expect mould creeping up the walls in every room if we don't find some way to get rid of it. A fungal pelt also covers the floor in two of the rooms, and part of the ceiling is caved in in another. That leaves four usable guest rooms, as long as we can cover up that mould. Hopefully the reviewer won't ask to see the others.

Aunt Kate has at least had some work done in the bathrooms. They're wet rooms – tiled across their floors and halfway up the walls, with a drain in the middle of the slightly sloping floor. But other than the new tiles, they're pure pre-war, which makes them so old that they've come all the way back around to retro.

There's a cistern high above the toilet and a claw-footed tub. The only concession to the last fifty years is the hand-held shower nozzle mounted on the wall.

I run the hot-water tap, waiting for it to heat. So far, so good. Gratefully I peel off my pyjamas and set my shampoo in the little tray at the far end of the tub. The round shower rail is bare, so maybe I'll see if Danny can find a plain curtain for it. Even with the door locked, I feel exposed without it.

The shampoo spikes my hair up into foamy peaks. The water must be softer here than in London. Maybe it's well water. Mmm. Lovely, clean Welsh well water. That could be a selling point to the guests, I suppose.

Suddenly the wall behind the bath moans like the undead are bricked up in there. Then something starts knocking on the wall, slowly at first, getting faster and faster and faster until....

'Jesus!'

The water scalds me before I can jump away. Shampoo bubbles slide into my eyes as I feel for the edge of the tub.

Ow ow ow ow.

Then there's a crash. Squinting through the stinging bubbles, I see the showerhead writhing on the floor beside the tub, soaking everything in its path.

I make a desperate lunge for the tap handles with my eyes streaming from the soap.

'Holy shit.'

'Mummy?' Mabel calls through the bathroom door. 'Can I have my shower now? I've used the loo already.'

Well, that explains the sudden change in water temperature. Our plumbing is going to poach our guests if we let them shower.

'Hang on, honey, let me rinse off and I'll draw you a bath instead.'

Mabel has found Mingus, who turns out to be a very rough-looking calico cat. He was asleep in the dining room cabinet where Aunt Kate keeps the white linen tablecloths (now covered in brown and black fur). She thinks Mingus loves her, just because he'll purr if she strokes him long enough. He does seem perfectly happy to be her new best friend, and I'm glad she's got the diversion. It's not easy always being the only little person in a grown-up world.

I stuff the tablecloths into the industrial size tumble dryer in the cellar. Hopefully most of the hair will come out in the filter. If not, we'll have to convince the guests that mohair tablecloths are the latest thing in the Snowdonian countryside.

I'm not fooling myself, by the way. Just so you know, I'm not delusional. We'll never get everything cleaned/arranged/painted/fixed in time. We'll have to prioritise. Starting with that mould. Aunt Kate must have planned for the rooms to be painted, so I send Danny to the guest bedrooms to see what he can do.

Meanwhile, I make a start on the downstairs hall, which looks even worse now that the newly cleaned windows let in all the daylight. In some places, the walls are so pitted that they look like they've been used for target practice. Painting over them will only give us freshly painted pockmarked walls.

Aunt Kate, what were you thinking, booking the reviewer in for Christmas? Did you really believe you'd get everything done in time for him to give you the rating you need?

I know the answer, even as I ask the question. Of course she did. Aunt Kate believes she can do anything she puts her mind to.

We're talking about the woman who opened a home for retired opera singers in northern Wales.

To be fair, that was Ivan's idea and, at first, it was his investment, too. She and Ivan were great friends from their touring days in Europe in the seventies, and they'd do anything for each other. When he retired, he wanted to give something back to the art that gave him so much.

Aunt Kate had always been a wandering soul, so why not move to Wales? They bought the house with some of his family money, and offered a home to ageing singers for nearly ten years. Tenants couldn't usually pay them anything, but at first, they were able to make ends meet using what was left of Ivan's savings, and then an equity release loan against the property.

The money ran out around the same time that Ivan's luck did. Aunt Kate nursed him through his final curtain call, and he left everything to her – the house, the land, and the unpaid equity release loan.

Which explains why I'm sitting in a crumbling house looking at the holes in the walls.

Danny shouts something from upstairs.

'Be right up.'

When I push open the bedroom door, it slams shut in my face.

'Don't come in!'

'Sorry. Are you painting the door?'

'Erm, yes? Oh, bugger.'

'Danny, what's going on? I'm coming in.'

It looks like the world's biggest seagull has taken aim at Danny. 'Spilled a bit of paint, did you?'

'A bit. Sorry. I'll try to be more careful.'

'Just see if you can get some on the walls, okay?'

'I'm not exactly a painting pro,' he says. 'Which is ironic, since I went to art school.'

'Did you really?'

'You don't have to sound so surprised. Yes, I did, really.'

'I'm sorry.' I stare at the walls. 'I guess I can see some Jackson Pollock influences in your work.'

'I stick to sculpture now,' he says. 'If I scrub the

mould off first and do just one coat, I should be able to finish the rooms by tomorrow. It will get mouldy again in a few weeks though if you don't fix the damp.'

'We just need to make everything hold together for a week. If we can pull this off then Aunt Kate can properly fix it later.'

'You mean we can stick everything together with chewing gum,' says Danny.

'Yes, exactly.' Hmm, chewing gum.

'Danny? Could we fill the holes in the walls downstairs with gum?'

He shakes his head. 'Nice idea, but no, that won't work. We tried it in our halls of residence to cover the nail holes we made in the plaster. It won't stick. Toothpaste is what you want for that.'

He goes back to his paintbrushes. I go to the bathroom to raid my sponge bag.

An hour later, I survey my handiwork. The wall smells minty fresh but it'll look okay with a coat of paint.

I'm even beginning to enjoy myself. With a bit of ingenuity and a lot more hard work, I feel like I'll honestly be able to tell Aunt Kate when I see her later that things are going to be all right.

CHAPTER FIVE

It's after midnight again before I crawl into Aunt Kate's bed with Mabel. I could move her into one of the other rooms once the stench of fresh paint wears off, but I'd rather keep her with me. I love reaching out in the night to stroke her soft hair and hear her rhythmic breathing on the pillow next to mine. I didn't know I could love someone this fiercely until I had her.

Aunt Kate always said she never wanted her own children (*What would I do with my own that I can't do with you, darling Lottie?*), but that's always made me a little sad. Then, after Mum and Dad died, selfishly I was glad. It meant that Mabel and I didn't have to share Aunt Kate's love with anyone else.

She stayed on to look after Mabel when I got back from Australia. I climbed off that plane and slept for two straight days. Aunt Kate quietly and efficiently took care of all the funeral arrangements, calling the friends and making all the administrative changes that a death involves.

After the funeral, as we sat together on the sofa, surrounded by Mum and Dad's many friends, she quietly asked me if I wanted her to stay.

'Would you?'

'Lions couldn't chase me away if you want me here.'

'Yes, please.'

She moved into Mum and Dad's room, and in those six months when she put her life on hold to help us learn to live ours again, she became as close to me as my own parents had been.

Now I'm going to do everything I can to help her.

Danny is already in the kitchen when I come downstairs the next morning. 'Day two,' he says. 'Do you want some tea?'

'I could murder a cup, thanks.' I wince at myself. At least Mabel-the-Mimic is still asleep. Being big sister to the cat is tiring work. I just hope she won't want to take him home with us.

Danny pours two large mugs and hands me one. As his hand brushes mine, he yanks it away like he's touched a hot burner. 'Sorry.'

Oh, come on, I think. So I've missed a few beauty appointments. I'm not hideous enough for *that* kind of reaction. Jeez.

But my frustration ebbs away with the first sips of hot milky tea as we sit across from each other at the long refectory table. I've got to say this for Aunt Kate.

Her house might be falling down, but she hasn't skimped on the décor. At least that gives us something to work with.

'I've cleaned out all the cabinets,' he tells me. 'Those mice do get around.'

'Uck. I thought cats were supposed to keep mice away. Yes, I'm talking about you, Mingus,' I tell him as he watches me from one of the kitchen chairs. 'You're not doing your job.'

He flicks his tail with a look of disdain on his whiskery face.

'Do you have everything here that you'll need for your cooking?'

'Sure,' Danny says. 'I can just make pasta every night, right?'

I laugh. 'Right. Imagine serving spag bol to a B&B critic. I've been thinking about that, actually. Last night I ordered some food that should give us everything we need to impress them. It's supposed to arrive by tomorrow lunchtime. You have no idea how hard it was to find a company that could deliver here.'

I spent two hours in the conservatory with my teeth chattering before finding an online shop called Posh Food Fast that can FedEx their food to us. 'We're not exactly within the Waitrose delivery area.'

'We're probably not even within the Lidl delivery area,' he says. 'Will you need me to get anything from the shops today?'

'I've made a list that should cover us for their whole stay.'

'Good, because everything will close tomorrow

afternoon and probably won't open until the 27th.'

'That's what I figured. Can you go into Rhyl today while Mabel and I visit Aunt Kate? You could do the shopping and then come back to collect us. I'll cook for us tonight after we get back from the hospital. I'd like to say thank you for helping me.'

Danny might be joking about the spag bol, but I'm not. Hopefully he likes pasta with Dolmio.

He shrugs. 'You've paid me a packet to do the cooking, but I'll accept your thanks too. Is there much left to do today?'

'Ha, what a naïve question. The answer is yes.' I pull the list from my bathrobe pocket. Where to start?

'I'm bored!' Mabel whines as I'm pulling all the dead weeds and flowers from the beds at the front of the house. My back aches and my arm muscles are screaming.

'Where's Mingus? I'm sure he'd like some company.'

'I can't find him.'

No surprise there. He lost his sense of humour when she tried combing his coat with her hairbrush.

'Go see if you can help Danny.'

'He sent me out here to help you.'

I smirk into the bushes. He's obviously dealt with children before. 'Okay, let me think a minute, and I can give you a job to do, okay?'

'A fun job?'

'Absolutely. Is there any other kind?'

Twenty minutes later, Mabel is surrounded by a sea of silver at the dining room table. There must be fifty pieces scattered around the house, from candlesticks and ornate candelabra to delicate mirrors, hairbrushes, sugar tongs and decorative boxes. You name it and someone covered it in silver and sold it to Aunt Kate.

I feel a bit bad as I kiss my daughter's forehead and leave her there with pots of silver polish. But someone will have to do it, and she does have those dexterous little fingers. Besides, it's not exploiting child labour when you've given birth to the labourer.

'Do you have lights or anything for the front?' Danny asks as I'm busy raking dead leaves from under the overgrown bushes. We haven't managed to find any clippers, so Mr Grey-Smythe and his family will have to accept our wild and rustic hedges. We dig up a load of blooming yellow primroses from the wood to fill out the bare spots in the borders. Hopefully they won't all die before Boxing Day.

'It would look a lot more Christmassy with lights,' he continues. 'You could have a ready-made Christmas tree right here.'

The tree!

'We don't have a tree for inside,' I say. 'We can't host guests for Christmas without a Christmas tree. Is it too late to order one?'

Danny stares at me. 'Order one? Is that how they do it in London?'

As if I don't feel foolish enough without admitting that my parents ordered our Christmas tree from the same delivery service for more than a dozen years.

'I suppose you'd just go chop one down in the forest then?'

'Exactly,' he says. 'Do you know where to find a saw?'

'In the garage, I guess.' My eye falls on the tree by the front door. 'Maybe we could cut this one down. It's a nice shape.'

'And leave the stump? I don't think your aunt would appreciate you chopping down her landscaping. We can find one in the wood.'

Mabel will love seeing a Christmas tree in its natural environment. It'll be like the time she first saw Brussels sprouts still on their stalk at the farmer's market. She had no idea that's how they grow. 'Give me two minutes. I'll just go get Mabel.'

We make a merry party half an hour later as we stomp along the woodland paths looking for two straight, tall trees for the parlour and the hall.

'Do you play jolly woodsman like this a lot?' I call to Danny as he walks a bit ahead with the saw slung over his shoulder. He seems at home amongst the trees, casual and relaxed and competent. I'm not used to that. My parents were lost if they had to do anything more complicated than changing a light bulb. And now I work with computer programmers. I haven't exactly been surrounded by manly displays of ability.

So Mabel isn't the only one impressed by this outing.

'Usually I'd work this week and next,' Danny says, 'so it's not worth bothering with a tree.'

'I guess a lot of people need taxis over the holidays.'

He shakes his head. 'I don't mean driving the taxi. I take two weeks off at the end of each year so that I can sculpt full-time.'

'A taxi driver with the soul of an artist.' I smile. 'Do you sell your sculptures and have exhibits and things like that?'

'Yeah, whenever I can. But it doesn't pay, so I fit it in around driving. Sculpting doesn't pay the bills yet. One day, maybe. What do you do for work?'

'Oh, it's boring. I'm a software programmer, mostly for games.'

His eyes light up. 'That doesn't sound boring. Do you like it?'

'I don't mind it. I guess it's only boring if you're not a gamer.'

'What about you? Are you a gamer?'

I shrug. Despite working in the industry for five years, the gaming bug never properly took hold. I much prefer curling up with a good book. The last thing I feel like doing after spending all day in front of a computer is stare at another screen.

'Mummy, look!' Mabel runs to a pretty pine and hugs it. 'Ouch.'

'I think that one might be a bit small.'

It's exactly Mabel's height.

'How about this one though?' I say of the one beside it. 'It looks straight. What do you think, Danny?'

'It's your job to choose and mine to saw. Say the word and it's ours.'

'Speaking of ours, are we trespassing? We are, aren't we?'

'Probably, but this is the kind of an emergency where trespassing's okay. Besides, who's around to stop us?'

He's right. There doesn't seem to be a soul for miles. It's completely silent here amongst the trees.

'So, will this be our Christmas tree?' He pulls the saw from his shoulder.

'I think so. It's tall enough. And that other one would work for the parlour.'

'Then stand back, ladies.'

Mabel springs to my side.

'Mabel,' he says. 'You've got the most important job. I'm going to saw and when you see it start to tip, you have to shout *timber*. Okay?'

She giggles.

'I'm not kidding. It's critical, so get ready.'

She giggles again and whispers, 'Tell me when, Mummy, okay, so I don't miss it?'

An hour later the Christmas trees are up in the hall and the parlour, thanks to Danny's handy homemade tree stands. They're bare of ornaments though.

'Let's have a look around for Aunt Kate's Christmas stash.'

I know she's got one. We've already found decorations for Easter, Valentine's Day and the Queen's

Jubilee squirrelled away in the many cabinets in the house. If the worst comes to the worst we can always drape the trees with bunting and call it a patriotic Christmas.

I don't believe in ghosts, but I swear this house retains some of the character of its past inhabitants. It's easy to imagine women of a certain age in full stage makeup and flowing gowns draped on the sofas and chaise longue while Ivan plays host, tipping ice cubes into gin and tonics.

Of course, they probably wore tracksuits to the Tesco and did Zumba in the conservatory, but I like my romantic vision better.

'Lottie, I've found them,' Danny calls as he staggers downstairs with a huge cardboard box. 'There's another one up there. It's not heavy, just awkward to carry. This one has the lights. If you want to check them, I'll go get the other box.'

Mabel and I begin plugging in each of the two dozen strings to make sure they work. Some are even for outside. Perfect.

'This should be enough for both trees,' I say, winding the first string around from the top.

'If we space them carefully,' Mabel adds.

I look at her. 'Do you remember Granddad saying that every year?'

'No, but you say it every year,' she says shyly. 'And then you say that Granddad always said it. Does it make you sad?'

'No, honey, it makes me happy to remember him.'

We've just got the lights on the first tree when Danny brings the other box down. 'Sorry for the delay, but I had to take a phone call.'

I keep forgetting that he has his own life outside Aunt Kate's B&B.

'I think we've got plenty of decorations,' he says. 'Some look like antiques.'

'I'm not surprised. Aunt Kate loves Christmas. She's going to be so unhappy to miss this one.'

I feel a little stab at my words. As I sat by her hospital bed last night, I kept wishing she'd open her eyes. No matter that I know she's on drugs that are keeping her in the coma. And that that's a good thing. She'll sleep as long as the doctors want her to.

'We'll have Christmas with her when she wakes up, won't we, Mummy?'

'Definitely, and she'll love how we've decorated the house. I bet it hasn't looked this good since— Can I see those, please, Mabel?'

She hands me the box of ornaments she's just picked up.

Oh, Mum.

It's an old-fashioned ornament box, the kind from the fifties or sixties, made of thin white cardboard with a crinkly cellophane window on the top and a dozen compartments for glass baubles. Whatever baubles once lived there are long gone though, replaced by others that were never a set.

They were my mother's.

Or duplicates at least. Every year, Mum bought a new ornament for our tree. The little wooden drummer boy, the blown-glass Christmas tree, the pom-pom snowman, they're all here. She must have bought two and sent one to Aunt Kate each year. After the accident, Celine made sure she packed ours away in a separate box at home. They've stayed in the attic for the last three Christmases. I wasn't ready to open up those memories.

Now, I guess, it's time to hang them again. 'Here, Mabel, you can put up the first one.'

Carefully she selects a branch for the silver angel. 'It's beautiful. Is it a guardian angel?'

'I think it must be,' I tell her.

CHAPTER SIX

I'm dead on my feet by the time Danny drives us back from the hospital that night. But a promise is a promise so, practically delirious, I stumble to the kitchen, over-boil the pasta, pour over a jar of sauce and, as a small apology for my cooking, make up a batch of elderflower and ginger cordial for us all.

'Mummy, don't come in yet!' Mabel calls from behind the closed dining room door.

I can hear her and Danny whispering together. That makes me smile. I guess I'd better do as I'm told.

I sit on the stairs to wait for my invitation inside. The hall isn't going to win any House Beautiful awards, but it's not bad for two days' hard graft. I just hope the toothpaste holds up in the walls.

'Okay, you can come i-i-i-nnn,' Mabel sings.

I let out a gasp when I see what they've been up to.

The dining room is gorgeous. Two twinkling silver

candelabra stand on the long sideboard against the back wall and pine boughs are tucked over the large gilded mirror above it. More boughs rest on the windowsills and the freshly washed panes reflect the candlelight back into the room. The middle of the long dining table is illuminated too.

'We didn't use the tablecloth in case I spill on it,' Mabel says.

'Or in case I spill on it,' Danny adds.

'Most likely it'd be me though, Danny. I am only seven.'

'You did a beautiful job. What a transformation,' I tell them.

Danny smiles. 'I think it looks good enough for the reviewer, don't you?'

'If he's not impressed with this then he's got a heart of stone.' My tummy fizzes with excitement. We're going to pull this off!

I pour the cordial into three cut-glass goblets and dish out our dinner. 'I'm sorry the food probably won't measure up to the surroundings, but I did warn you that cooking isn't my forte. That's why I'm paying you. Cheers.' I clink Mabel's glass beside me and Danny's across from us. 'At least I know how to make good drinks.'

'This is delicious,' he says. 'Elderflower?'

'Yes, and ginger. If I'd remembered the lime I'd have added that. I'm glad you're impressed with the drinks. Remember that when you taste my cooking.'

'Oh, I'm sure it's not bad.' He takes a forkful. 'Hmm. Well. The drinks are good anyway.'

Mabel catches my eye. 'I think it's just fine, Mummy, thank you.'

'Mabel,' Danny says, reddening. 'Where are my manners? Thank you, Lottie, for dinner. Everything is great.'

'Liar,' I say. 'But thank you.'

'Pants on fire,' murmurs Mabel into her spaghetti.

I feel a jolt as I watch Mabel chatting easily with Danny as we all finish our plates. When I was first pregnant, I worried a lot about being a single mother. But when we moved in with Mum and Dad those worries faded. Mabel got to have two extra people who loved her. Aside from the occasional questions about her father, she doesn't seem to mind our modern family arrangement.

But maybe she is missing something.

As if reading my mind, Mabel says, 'Mummy, is Aunt Kate married?'

'No, she was never married.'

'But what about Uncle Ivan?'

Ivan died before Mabel was born, so she's never met him. But Aunt Kate always talks about him like he's still around. 'They were very dear friends, but they weren't married. Uncle Ivan was a confirmed bachelor.'

'What's that?'

'It just means he wasn't the marrying kind.'

'Danny, are you the marrying kind?'

'Mabel,' I warn. Our financial arrangement doesn't give us the right to pry into Danny's personal life.

'No, I've never been married.' He forks in another

mouthful of spaghetti. He's a good sport. 'I guess nobody'd have me.'

I find that hard to believe, but Mabel seems to consider this. 'I guess nobody'd have Mummy either.'

Danny tries to cover his laugh with a cough.

She's not wrong though. Her father didn't stick around for very long after I dropped the bombshell on him. I was heartbroken at the time, but we probably wouldn't have worked out anyway.

I've got to give him some credit though. He might have bolted from our relationship but he did try to be a dad, of sorts. He was a hit-or-miss presence in our lives for the first few years after Mabel was born. I did want her to know her father, even though every time he visited it opened the wound in my heart again. And Mabel wasn't overly keen on him. As a toddler, she didn't understand why this strange bloke sometimes visited, expecting her to welcome him. His visits became more awkward over time, until finally they stopped.

So, after wishing at first that we could be a family, it was actually a relief by the time he moved to Thailand and left Mabel and me to get on with our lives. Knowing him, he's probably living in a beach hut with a string of young women that he updates more often than he does his Facebook status.

'I do have a daughter though,' Danny says. 'She's eight and she lives all the way over in America.'

Ah, that explains why he's so good with Mabel.

'Is she like me?'

'Well, she is smart like you, and nice and pretty,

so yes, I guess she is.'

'But she doesn't live with you?'

'Mabel, you must be getting tired,' I say, seeing the sadness in Danny's eyes. 'If you're finished eating, let's get your teeth cleaned, okay? I'll come back down in a few minutes to help with the dishes.'

'That's okay,' Danny says, stacking the plates. 'I can clear up and make us some tea.'

By the time I tuck Mabel into bed and get back to the dining room, Danny has laid the table with pretty teacups and saucers.

'Mabel is great,' he says, pouring out a cup for each of us.

'She has her moments.' I sigh. 'She can really get on my nerves sometimes. Does it make me a bad mother to say that? Sometimes when I listen to everyone else talking about how perfect their children are, I do wonder if I'm just less maternal, or if mine really is a pain in the arse.'

Danny smiles. 'She's just precocious because she's clever and, no, that doesn't make you a bad mother. People who act like their children can do no wrong are kidding themselves. Nobody's perfect.'

This makes me feel a little less guilty. Ah, guilt, every parent's constant companion. 'She is a good kid at heart and she hasn't always had it easy. My parents died three years ago. That was awful for her. For all of us.'

'That's really shite, I'm sorry,' he says. 'I lost my granddad last year. I know it's not the same thing as a parent, but we were very close. That's his taxi outside.

He taught me to drive. I know I should get a decent car, but it reminds me of him.'

I'm not about to comment on his deceased grandad's teaching skills. Far be it for me to speak ill of the dead.

'Grief is grief when you love someone,' I say instead. 'It's a little easier for us now. Aunt Kate was amazing at the time. She came to live with us right after it happened. That's why, now...'

'I understand,' he says. 'But you said she's recovering.'

I'm desperate not to dwell in the shadowy corners of my imagination so, instead, I nod. 'Tell me about your daughter.'

She lives in Austin, Texas, he says, where her mother is from. She's an artist too, that Danny met at university. I can't help thinking that his story has a lot in common with mine and Mabel's. I wonder if Mabel's father ever misses her like Danny obviously misses his daughter.

'Do you get to see her?'

He fiddles with the handle on his teacup. His big hands look ill-suited to such a delicate object.

'I go over as often as I can get the money together for a flight. Her mother is good about me visiting. She was the one who wanted to move back to the US when Phoebe was two. Otherwise I'd see her more often.'

'So, you're not together with Phoebe's mother because of the distance?'

'Oh no,' he laughs. 'We're not together because

we drove each other mad. She thought I was too intense, and she's probably right. But she never took anything seriously. We rowed all the time. Phoebe was definitely the best thing about our relationship. Luckily she got the right balance from both of us.' He sighs. 'I'm dying to see her again.'

I can't imagine being away from Mabel for weeks or months at a time. 'When will you go next?'

'Right after Christmas, thanks to you.'

Ah, so that's why he's taken up my offer.

'Then it was lucky I came along.'

'Very lucky.'

As we sit drinking our tea, a low rumble starts behind the dining room's back wall.

'That must be the 8.30 train. Cook mentioned it,' I say, checking my watch. 'Right on time.'

The teacups begin to rattle in their saucers as the train closes in on us. It sounds like it's about to come through the house.

White flecks start raining down on the table. They look like an awful case of dandruff against the dark wood. But as the train passes, bigger pieces start bouncing off the polished table top. Then a chunk the size of a fifty pence piece splashes into my teacup.

'That ceiling's gonna come down,' Danny says with his arms over his head.

As the sound recedes I survey the debris strewn everywhere. 'I don't think my toothpaste is going to help much here. Danny, we can't let the reviewer go through that every night. What'll we do? The only other place to eat is in the kitchen... I don't suppose we could we make a chef's table there and let them watch you cook?'

He looks horrified. 'No way! I mean we've got to have Christmas dinner in here. Otherwise it's not very Christmassy. The ceiling only seems to come loose because of the train. We'll just have to keep them out of here when it passes. Otherwise the house looks fine.'

The list of things we need to hide from the reviewer is getting longer than those we want to show him.

This is pretty hopeless. 'It might look fine,' I say. 'As long as we don't let anyone take a shower, or sit in here or try using their mobile inside the house.'

I'm kidding myself. The reviewer isn't going to judge the house on cosmetics alone. It's got to meet all his needs. Surely, it's not too much to expect to dine in a dining room.

I wish Aunt Kate were here. She'd know what to do.

'We're never going to pull this off,' I tell Danny. 'There's too much wrong with the house.'

'What would your aunt say?'

I laugh. 'She'd say "Come on, girl, if at first you don't succeed, then try, try again. Rome wasn't built in a day" And she'd be right. It's worse not to at least try.'

Come on, Lottie, I tell myself. You're a programmer. You *know* there's got to be an answer if you think logically.

'Maybe if we think of everything that could be a problem and then find a way around those things, there'll still be a chance,' I tell Danny. 'Starting with that flippin' train. It's nice in here when it's not shaking down the plaster, so why can't we serve a big lunch instead, and have sandwiches and tea in the parlour in the evening?'

We've just got to stop thinking about what we can't do, and think about what we *can*.

'And all the bathrooms have those gorgeous bathtubs,' I point out. 'The guests could use those instead of showering. Could you take the shower extensions off the taps, and maybe get the mounts off the walls? I think we've got enough extra toothpaste to fill the holes. Then at least if someone flushes, nobody will die.'

'You could tell everyone that mobile phones are restricted to the conservatory,' Danny suggests. 'Make it sound like it's in keeping with the ambience. I can make sure the fire is always lit in there so that it's warm.'

'This is all starting to sound like a Victorian house,' I say. 'We just need servants running up and down the back stairs tugging their forelocks and curtsying.'

'That's us,' Danny reminds me.

'Oh yeah.'

Wait a minute... 'Why *couldn't* we make this a Victorian Christmas? I mean officially. We're practically there anyway.'

Then we brush the debris from the table and stay in the dining room until after midnight again, working through all the details.

CHAPTER SEVEN

Mabel comes downstairs on Christmas Eve morning wearing her favourite blue tutu. I've been up for hours already trying to find enough duvets that aren't coated in Mingus hair. I did find extra candlesticks and candles to put some in each room. We're going to stretch the Victorian theme as far as we possibly can. If I find any brass bed-warmers or stocking caps, I'm definitely laying them out for our guests.

'You look beautiful, Mabel.'

'Well, we have to look our best for our guests, don't we?'

I stare down at myself. My jeans are covered with paint. Mould and lord-knows-what-else streak my once-white top. Even if I could get them clean, Mabel is right. I don't look fit to be a twenty-first century B&B host, let alone a Victorian lady.

Unfortunately, when I'd shoved clothes into my bag at three a.m. to come here, I wasn't thinking about impressing a B&B reviewer and his family.

'Morning,' she says to Danny, who's on his knees in the hall rubbing the floorboards with tan shoe polish. There was no floor varnish amongst Aunt Kate's paint pots, but for some reason she's got a big box full of shoe polish. Danny is touching up the spots where we had to clean up his paint splatters with nail varnish remover.

For someone who claims to be a sculptor, his hand-eye coordination isn't great.

'Can we have scrambled eggs this morning?' Mabel asks.

'Sure we can, if we've got eggs.' He looks at me for confirmation.

Oh god, I've forgotten all about the chickens!

'I've just got to quickly check something outside, okay? Mabel, do you think Mingus is awake yet?'

While my daughter rushes off to find that poor cat, I scurry outside, praying I haven't accidentally starved Aunt Kate's flock.

The back garden is as wild and overgrown as the front was before we took the rakes to it. The hedges are growing willy-nilly and the uncut grass is flattened and streaked brown. It looks grim, but we don't have time now for any more gardening.

Our guests are due at two pm.

My feet squelch in the wet undergrowth as I stomp to the crumbling garage, behind which I spot the chicken run. The hen house is at one end, but I don't see any hens.

Creeping into the pen, and bracing myself for the

worst, I peek into the hut's doorway.

Two dozen beady eyes stare me down as the birds erupt into a chorus of clucks and squawks. I can't really blame them. I'd be cross too if I'd been ignored for three days. Those are definitely angry birds.

I hurry back to the house.

'Hey, Danny, I don't suppose you know anything about chickens?'

'I know how to eat them,' he says.

'It might come to that if our food doesn't get delivered today. Cook said *Don't forget the chickens* in her email. I assume that means they lay eggs and need feeding. Could you please go see if there are any eggs? They're just out back behind the garage.'

'If you were just out there the why didn't you...?'

'I had a quick look, but they seemed angry.'

'You're not frightened of chickens.'

'Really angry. Watch your eyes. They go for the eyes.'

He shakes his head, mumbling, 'Who's afraid of chickens?'

He's back ten minutes later, his eyes and entrails intact. 'The chickens aren't man-eaters, for the record. They're fed, and look what we've got!'

I peer into his basket. 'Are those supposed to be eggs?'

Some are round, some oblong, others as tiny as grapes.

'Better not let the ladies hear you say that. They're very proud of their efforts.'

I shouldn't make fun. It's not like I can lay any

myself. They'll have to do. The shops in the village will be closed for Christmas by now anyway.

Danny goes, whistling, to the kitchen to cook us an omelette.

The FedEx driver turns up just before noon, as grumpy as those in London always seem to be. But at least Posh Food Fast hasn't let us down.

Danny looks over my shoulder while I unpack the bags. 'Mmm, look at this!' I say.

'Tinned tuna?'

'Psh, you need glasses. It's caviar! I wasn't sure if they'd be able to get it. It was out of stock on the website. Ooh, and look at this beef.'

There's also a whole salmon and smoked salmon and kippers and Christmas pudding. My mouth is watering just thinking of the feast ahead. Not that we'll be eating with the guests, being the hired help. But good food is good food even when it's leftovers enjoyed in the kitchen. Mabel and I, and Danny too, of course, are going to have a very tasty Christmas.

'We can offer oatmeal or cooked breakfast in the mornings, okay?' I tell him. 'I can write up a little menu to hand out. That'd be a nice touch. And I thought we could have the salmon for dinner today and the beef for tomorrow. Maybe you can make some kind of sauce to go with the salmon, and do something special with the carrots and potatoes. We've got lots of bread for sandwiches later. You'll do them with the crusts cut off, right?'

'Erm, all right, if you want. How do I cook the

salmon?'

'However you like. You're the chef! I'm just going to check on Mabel and get out of these clothes before everyone arrives. I'll let you make a start. We should probably eat around three.'

After making Mabel and Danny triple-promise and cross their hearts not to flush the loo, I have a quick shower. Then I survey my suitcase for the millionth time. But my choices haven't improved in the night. I've got only jeans, tee shirts and a few worse-for-wear jumpers.

Rupert Grey-Smythe and his family will just have to overlook my appearance. I can't magic up an outfit out of thin air...

Although maybe there's something in Aunt Kate's closet. She's bigger than me, but if she's got a dress that won't make me look like a sixty-year-old B&B owner, it'll do.

My heart sinks when I fling open her closet doors. There are loads of wide legged trousers and long colourful tunics, but not a single dress.

Unless Mabel lets me borrow her tutu, I'll have to make do with what's in the closet. A belt will at least hold up the trousers. At worst, there's clothesline downstairs.

The closet is bigger than just its double doors. It runs along the entire length of the wall.

I get my phone out and shine the light into its murky depths.

What greets me takes my breath away.

'Danny! Mabel, come up here!' I call to them

from the top of the stairs.

I haul the tunics and trousers off the rails and fling them onto the bed.

Mabel's got Mingus clasped to her chest as she runs in. Danny's not far behind.

'What do you think of these?' I point my phone again into the dark closet.

Danny whistles. 'I think your Aunt Kate is one interesting lady.'

Aunt Kate's opera frocks, made of rich dark velvets and silks, are a bit wrinkled but unbelievably beautiful. There must be a dozen tucked into the back of her closet.

And it seems she wasn't the only singer to be paid in clothes. Ivan's knee breeches and embroidered waistcoat are big for Danny, but the clothesline will sort him out.

'You look like a princess!' cries Mabel as I do up the scarlet silk dress.

Yes, a princess in trainers. Aunt Kate wasn't paid in shoes, it seems. The only alternatives to my Nikes are her sturdy orthopaedic walking shoes with Velcro fasteners.

I drape a deep purple embroidered shawl over Mabel's small shoulders. 'I'm sorry the dresses are all too big for you. Would you like to wear this?'

'It's okay, Mummy,' she says, accepting the shawl. 'This looks nice with my tutu.'

'You both look good,' Danny says. 'Whereas I feel like a prat.' He pulls at his billowing white ruffled sleeves. 'And I'm not sure this is Victorian either.'

Maybe not, but his long wavy dark hair and the way the neck of his shirt is gathered closed with another ruffle beneath his stubbled chin makes him look very olden times. So what if we're off by a century or so? 'Oh, come now, you could be Caruso himself,' I tease.

He doesn't look too sure. 'Except I can't sing for toffee. I might pass for a very quiet extra at the back of the stage.'

The clock in the hall gongs two just as Mabel shouts 'They're here!' from the parlour window where she's been watching the driveway. 'They've got a lot of bags.'

Danny and I go out to greet them.

'Mr Grey-Smythe?' I look between the two men taking luggage out of the boot. Mabel's right. It's a lot for just two days.

'Yes, that's me. Please call me Rupert.' The taller man shakes my hand as he stares at the front of the house. 'Are you Kate?'

'Oh, no, I'm not. I'm her niece, Lottie Crisp. It's a pleasure to meet you. Unfortunately, my aunt has been in an accident and she's not able to be here.'

His brow creases with concern. 'I'm sorry to hear that. I hope she's all right?'

'Yes, she'll be okay, thanks.'

'Did I miss a memo somewhere?' he asks, tearing his eyes away from the discoloured walls of our B&B to scan my dress.

'Ah, yes, well. Welcome to your Victorian

Christmas!'

I bob into a little curtsey like they do on Downton Abbey.

'Sorry about the front of the house. The, erm, builders cancelled on my aunt. She's furious about it, naturally. This is Danny, our chef.'

Danny just nods. 'Can I help you with your bags?' he asks.

'Thank you, yes. Hugo, leave those,' Rupert says to the other bloke. 'The man will get them.'

Rupert strides toward the front door as I hurry to beat him to it.

His nose twitches as he enters the hall.

'It smells of shoe polish,' he says.

'Erm, yes, it's a complimentary service. You can leave your shoes outside your door in the evening and we'll polish them. We'll take care of everything for you here.'

I stick my hand out to the forty-something slender woman who comes up behind us. She hasn't cracked a smile since she turned up. 'Yes, well, as I said, welcome to your Victorian Christmas. I'm Lottie.'

She doesn't bother making eye contact when she speaks. 'Prunella, Rupert's sister.' She waves her hand at the others. 'These are my twins, Oscar and Amanda, and my husband, Hugo.'

The children look around Mabel's age. Both are pale and slim like their parents. In fact, Prunella and Hugo could be twins themselves, with their beaky noses, close-set watery blue eyes and very high foreheads. Rupert, on the other hand, though slender like his sister, is darker, with strong features that assemble into a pleasing, if austere, face.

Hugo scans me up and down as he offers me his soft damp hand.

'Have you got Sky?' Prunella asks.

'No, I'm sorry, there's no television.'

'Mother!' says Oscar, glaring at me. 'How are we supposed to watch *Bad Santa* without a TV?'

'Never mind, darling, we'll watch it on the computer. You do have fast broadband, right?'

Her look dares me to disappoint her again.

'Yes, in the conservatory.'

'Rupert,' she whines, 'I told you this would be the middle of nowhere.'

'I suppose it's meant to be rustically charming, Pru.'

It's not the start I'd hoped for. 'It will be charming,' I tell them, 'but I promise you it won't be rustic.'

'We'll make the best of it, Pru,' says Hugo.

'Oh, do shut up, Hugo, you always say that. I want a bath now. We've been travelling all day to get here. Where's my room? Have him bring my luggage.'

Danny is just struggling in with all the bags.

'I'll show you upstairs then,' I tell them. 'Your rooms are all together on the first floor. You're going to love our bathtubs. As part of the service, we'll run your baths for you, so that all you'll have to do is step into the soothing water when you're ready. After all, ladies and gentlemen didn't prepare their own baths in Victorian days. There's a button in each of your rooms by the door that rings a bell in the kitchen. Just press that whenever you want anything and someone will be right up.'

These aren't the people I'd choose for Mabel and I to share our Christmas with but, I have to remind myself, we're doing all this for Aunt Kate.

'Whew,' I say when I get back to the kitchen after drawing Prunella's bath. Danny is pulling food from the fridge and larder. 'This is going to be hard work. Is everything under control here?'

'Controlled chaos, thanks.' He wipes his brow. Pots are boiling away on the hob and the work surfaces are strewn with a mass vegetable suicide.

'Okay, if you're sure.'

The bell for Hugo and Prunella's room tinkles.

'I'm so sorry I told them about those service buttons. I'll go see what they want.'

Upstairs I knock on the closed door.

'Come in,' I hear Hugo call.

'Hi, did you want something?'

He's lying on the bed in his bathrobe.

'Oh, excuse me,' I say, stopping in my tracks.

'Ah, Lottie, yes. I wondered if I could have a brandy? I'd like to relax while Prunella is in the bath. She'll be ages in there.'

'I'll check downstairs. Dinner will be in about an hour. You can go down to the dining room whenever you'd like. Is that all right?'

'Yes, that's fine. Oh, and please don't think my wife is ungrateful. Today is just a bad day. We're very much looking forward to our stay, and I do appreciate your costumes. Very much. Yes,' he says, his eyes flickering to my chest. 'Very much.'

'I'll see if I can find that brandy.'

And maybe some pepper spray.

Talk about creepy. I hate to think what he'll be like after a few drinks...

Drinks. Oh no. I haven't. Have I? I have.

I can't believe I forgot to put wine on Danny's shopping list. Or brandy or anything stronger than the elderflower cordial we had last night.

I hurry back down to the kitchen. 'Danny, you haven't run across a stash of wine, have you? Or spirits? Anything?'

'No, why?'

'Because I completely forgot to get any alcohol.'

Of course they'll want to drink. It's Christmas. They'll need alcohol just to put up with each other.

'How could you forget alcohol?' He brushes a lock of his unruly hair out of his eyes.

'Because I don't drink.'

The thought of taking even a sip, after that drunk driver turned my world upside down, makes me feel queasy.

'Hugo has already asked for brandy. They're going to expect wine, at the very least. The shops are closed now, aren't they?'

I know the answer.

'Well,' he says. 'I do have something at home, but you may not like it.'

'It doesn't really matter if I like it, as long as we've got booze for the guests.'

'Then I can run home and get a few bottles. You've still got lots of that cordial, right? We'll use that to cut the— as mixers. Can you please keep an eye on the potatoes, and take them off the heat when they're ready?'

'Sure thing. Thanks, Danny.'

At least you can't overcook potatoes.

CHAPTER EIGHT

'You've overcooked the potatoes,' Danny says half an hour later, poking the mush with a fork. 'Did you check the carrots?'

'You didn't say anything about the carrots.'

He frowns when he peers into the pot. 'I guess I can add enough butter and salt to make up for it.' Holding up a green bottle, he adds, 'By the time they get through this, they won't be able to taste anything anyway.'

'What is it?' There's no label on the bottle.

'This is gin.' He pulls another bottle from his bag. 'And this is brandy. Just make sure you always serve it in very small quantities. Whatever you do, never leave the bottle with the guests.'

'And why aren't the bottles labelled?'

'I don't bother with that. I know which is which.'

'As long as it doesn't blind anyone.'

'My eyesight is perfect.'

'Then let's mix one with the cordial.'

I start pouring the gin into the pitcher I used for our drinks last night, but Danny grabs my hand.

'Hey, hey, stop. You'll kill them. Seriously, you need about a spoonful for each glass, that's all. You'd better let me do it.'

Everyone is waiting for lunch in the dining room. Prunella's bath didn't help her mood, and the twins are rocking back and forth in their chairs, trying to see who can break theirs first. At least Hugo has his clothes on.

'Here we are!' I say.

The tureens of mash and carrots – which are also mash – are heavy in my arms.

A very nervous-looking Danny comes in behind me with the steaming main course.

'We'll leave you to enjoy your lunch, but do let us know if you need anything. Would everyone like a drink? There's also a non-alcoholic cordial for the children.'

'Where's the wine?' Prunella asks.

'Oh, well, we've made a special drink instead, and it's really delicious.'

'The Victorian landed gentry loved this at Christmas,' Danny says as he pours glasses of moonshine for everyone.

Hugo nods like he knows this already.

'Thank you,' says Rupert. 'We'll let you know if we need anything.'

I fight the urge to curtsey. It's the flippin' dress.

'Wait a second,' says Hugo. 'Is that prosciutto wrapped around the salmon?'

'No, it's also salmon,' says Danny, looking at me as if to say *What kind of nutter wraps salmon in prosciutto?*

My look glares back: What kind of nutter wraps salmon in more salmon?!

'Ah, yes, our salmon-in-salmon recipe,' I say, instead of what I'm thinking. That smoked salmon was supposed to be for another meal. 'We've researched the menus of the era and were surprised at some of them too, but they're authentic.' My face reddens. They can't really believe such nonsense.

But Hugo is already downing his gin cordial and Prunella has her fingers on her temples. Something tells me she has a lot of bad days.

'And here's the gravy!' Mabel says, setting it on the table.

'Gravy on salmon?' Rupert asks, pouring a bit on the side of his plate. 'Beef?'

'It's good on the mash,' the girl twin, Amanda, says, talking with her mouth full. 'It tastes like Mother's.'

'Bisto?' I mouth at Danny.

'And I suppose the carrots are pureed like this because Victorians lost their teeth early,' Rupert says.

That sounds at least as good as the excuse I'm about to come up with.

'Hmm, I'm not sure I've got a Victorian palate,' he continues. 'But I do appreciate the effort. Thank you.'

We all rush out before they can ask any more

questions.

'You used all the smoked salmon?' I hiss to Danny when we're safely back in the kitchen.

'You said to cook the salmon.'

'You don't *cook* smoked salmon. You eat it as it is. That was supposed to be for tea one night.'

'I wouldn't eat that as it was. It looked slimy and raw.'

I'm starting to doubt Danny's culinary skills, but considering that I've made baby food of the veg, I'm no better.

Upstairs later, the tile floor is soaking wet from Prunella's bath, and her towel is in a heap beside the loo. The messy cow.

As I mop the floor, I hope the family aren't going to take too many baths. I know the twins won't. They're the same age as Mabel and she acts like soap and water might kill her.

We've just got time to run to the hospital to see Aunt Kate before we need to serve tea, so we leave everyone in the parlour with stacks of board games and newspapers. The twins forgot their fury over the lack of telly as soon as they caught sight of Mingus. That poor, poor cat.

Danny stays behind to boil the eggs for sandwiches, throwing me his car keys.

'Just don't hit anything, please,' he adds after telling me the trick to coaxing the car out of third gear.

'How is she?' I ask Dr Lonergan at the hospital when she comes in to Aunt Kate's room. 'Any better?'

She smiles. 'Yes, in fact. I want to keep her on the medication for another day or so, and then we should be able to reverse the coma.'

'Can you tell yet about possible brain damage?'

'All the tests we've run look clear, so that's a good sign. How are you holding up?'

Her concern threatens to undo me. But I haven't got time for a meltdown now. 'I'm fine. The guests have arrived at the house, so it's been a little crazy.'

'It's going to be fine, Aunt Kate,' I say, in case she can hear me. I take her hand. 'They're all settled in and they've had their lunch. You don't have to worry, okay? Just rest so you can get better.'

I squeeze her hand, remembering too late that she can't squeeze back.

We make it back to the B&B without stalling the car. If Danny has any money left over from his ticket to America, he might think about upgrading it from death trap to just a load of junk.

The hard-boiled eggs are cooling in a bowl beside the sink. I slice into the first one. Chalky green yolks spill out.

'Danny, how long did you boil the eggs?'

'Not long. Half an hour or so. Are they cooked?'

'Oh, they're cooked.' We can use them to defend the house against invaders if we need to. 'Mabel has rubber balls that wouldn't bounce as well.'

'I didn't want to under-cook them.'

'Mission accomplished.' Unless the hens are working overtime, there won't be enough for a second batch. 'Let me think.'

We've got to have something to feed everyone for tea. I haven't the faintest idea how to bake and, judging by Danny's efforts so far, neither has he. That leaves sandwiches, but with no smoked salmon and now no eggs, what are we supposed to make?

The bell over the door rings. They must have found the button in the parlour.

'The Master calls, I tell Danny. 'I'll be right back. Meanwhile try to think of something we can use for sandwiches.'

'Sure,' he says. 'Is it okay if I run home quickly?'

'Have you got something at home that we could use?'

He frowns. 'I'm a bachelor living alone. We can't make Pot Noodle sarnies.'

'Right. You may as well do whatever you need to do at home. You don't have to be back here for an hour. I'll try to think of something.'

Prunella is lying on one of the sofas in front of the fire with her hand over her eyes, whilst the twins take turns throwing the Yahtzee dice at each other from five paces.

'Is everything all right?'

'I have a splitting headache,' says Prunella. 'Have

you got any tablets?'

'Sure, I'll just go get them.'

'Bring in some more of that drink, will you?' Hugo asks. 'Actually, I can help you carry the glasses.'

He hops up from the chair, swaying slightly as he does so.

'Hugo, I'm sure she's perfectly capable of carrying a tray by herself. Honestly, it *is* what she does.'

It's not worth pointing out that what I *do* is design gaming software for brats like hers.

'To tell the truth, I don't mind getting away from the family for a while,' Hugo says as he follows me to the kitchen. 'We were supposed to go to Tanzania, and they're still angry with Rupert for bringing us to Wales instead. But it's his dosh, so I can't really blame him for choosing a free holiday over one that'd cost a packet.'

'Free?' Aunt Kate doesn't charge very much for her rooms, but they aren't free.

'All expenses paid by your aunt,' Hugo says. 'I guess that's because she needs the rating.'

Brilliant. Not only are we killing ourselves to please these pompous arses, we're doing it for free.

I can feel him come up behind me as I reach into the cabinet for glasses. He's standing way too close. This is a rural kitchen, not a rush-hour Tube train.

Just as I'm about to grind my heel into his foot, Aunt Kate pops into my head. If she has waived the expenses for Rupert's whole stay, then it tells me just how much she feels she needs his rating. As much as I'd love to break Hugo's foot, I can't throw away her only chance.

He grasps the counter on either side of me as I turn with the glasses. 'I couldn't help but notice the way you looked at me earlier,' he says.

Yes, with utter contempt.

'I'm sorry, I—'

'Ssh, you don't have to be sorry.'

As his blubbery lips dart towards mine, I get a whiff of his foul breath.

'Jesus!' he shouts, with his upper lip clenched between my teeth.

Oh my god. I've bitten the reviewer's brother-in-law.

But then he smiles (when I release his lip) and shrugs. 'Oh, I see, you like to play hard to get.'

I catch a movement over Hugo's shoulder.

'I didn't mean to interrupt.'

Rupert is standing in the doorway, watching us.

CHAPTER NINE

Hugo springs back at the sound of his brother-in-law's voice. 'No, I don't think there's anything in your eye,' he says. 'I can't see anything.'

'Thanks. Actually, it feels better now.'

My heart is hammering.

'Would you like a drink, Rupert?' I ask.

'No, thank you. I was just checking on when tea would be ready. I've got some work to do.'

'Would seven be all right? We'll serve it in the parlour. I've just got to get some headache tablets for Prunella.'

I rush from the kitchen, leaving the two men staring each other down.

What must Rupert think? They've been here less than three hours and I've just rounded off an afternoon of bathtub gin and a questionable lunch with a romantic interlude in the arms of his sister's husband.

Unless one of his rating categories includes staff

promiscuity, I've put Aunt Kate's livelihood in jeopardy.

'Are you okay?' Danny asks when he returns at six on the dot. 'You look weird.'

Humiliation is coursing through me. I don't want to tell Danny what happened in the kitchen.

'I'm fine. I think this corset is too tight, that's all. I've been thinking about the sandwich situation. We can serve some of the caviar for the adults and make peanut butter and jam sandwiches for the twins. Aunt Kate has a jar of it in the larder, and Mabel goes nuts for the stuff, so I'm sure the twins will love it.'

'That doesn't sound very Victorian,' he points out.

'We can't be perfect. At least they won't go hungry. Just toast the bread for the caviar. With a little lemon, it'll be great. Very decadent. I'll make another batch of drinks.'

We're going to need it. Maybe if Hugo drinks enough, he'll pass out before he can lunge at me again.

'I've got to turn down everyone's beds while they're all downstairs, and restock the bathrooms. You're okay making the sandwiches and the tea?'

He nods, already counting out slices of bread.

It's only taken a few hours for the parlour to look like a bomb's hit it. The twins have pulled nearly every book from the shelves. The cushions are off the sofas and chairs and Oscar is throwing the Monopoly money in the air to watch it rain down over everything.

Danny noses the tea trolley through the door.

'Look, darlings, tea!' Hugo says. He seems to have forgotten his earlier sexual assault, but I'm pleased to see that his lip is swollen. Prunella hasn't noticed, but then she hasn't really paid him any attention since they arrived.

Rupert is staring at the trolley.

'Is everything okay?' I ask before I can stop myself. What if he outs me, like a real-life edition of Cluedo? *It was Ms Crisp in the kitchen with a romantic embrace.*

'I was just remembering my Granny's tea trolley. It looked just like that.'

I bet it had better food though.

'Do you remember it, Prunella?'

'I remember that she stank,' she says, shifting to a sitting position. 'I don't know why you insist on deifying her, Rupert.'

'I don't deify her, Pru, I just have good memories of being with her. Maybe if you let yourself feel anything but dissatisfaction, you would, too.'

'You can be ridiculous sometimes. I'll just have a cup of tea,' she says to me. 'White. I'm not hungry after that lunch.'

'Of course,' I say, pouring her a cup and wishing they wouldn't bicker in front of "the help". 'Would everyone like tea?'

'I'll have some more of that cocktail, if there's any going,' Hugo says.

I'm not about to leave the safety of the parlour again. 'Danny, could you please make a pitcher?'

'What's this?' Amanda demands as she picks up a sandwich.

'It's peanut butter and jam,' I say. 'My daughter loves them and I thought...'

Her tongue darts into the side of the sandwich. 'Yuck, I hate it!' She throws it back on the plate.

'I hate it too!' cries Oscar, without even trying a bite. 'I'm not eating it.'

'You don't have to eat it, darlings. They'll make whatever you want.'

'Well actually...'

'Do you want to try a special one?' Danny says smoothly as he returns with a fresh pitcher of blinding cocktail. 'Children aren't usually allowed to have these. But since it's Christmas I think you could...' He seems to reconsider. 'Well, maybe you're not ready for one.'

'Yes, I want one!' says Oscar.

'Me too, give it to me now!'

Danny sighs. 'Well, all right, but you're very lucky.' He hands a sandwich from the second plate to each child.

What are those?

Amanda and Oscar look unsure as they sniff the toasted bread. Then Amanda, in her trademark move, sticks her tongue into the side. Her eyes widen. She prises open the sandwich and licks it clean before throwing the spittle-slicked toast back on the plate.

'I want another one.'

Oscar levers his sandwich open. 'Me, too. I like it!'

Well, at least they'll get to eat something.

'I'll just go get the caviar,' I say.

'But it's right there,' Danny says. 'In the sandwiches.'

Amanda and Oscar are licking all the caviar out of the sandwiches.

'I'm impressed,' says Hugo, leering at my chest again. 'They're usually very fussy eaters. It looks like we'll need more sandwiches.'

Sighing, I go to the kitchen to make a hundred quid's worth of caviar into sandwiches for greedy children.

Rupert follows me.

'Lottie, may I have a quiet word please?'

'Listen, Rupert, that wasn't what you—'

'It's about the stockings,' he says.

I'm not wearing stockings, so he can't possibly be taking issue. Is he one of those sexist men who think women deserve what they get just because they're not dressed in floor-length potato sacks?

'Just what are you implying?'

'I'm not implying anything. Your aunt told me she'd have stockings for the children's gifts tonight. If you give them to me, please, I can put them in Prunella's room.'

Of course, it's Christmas Eve. I've got a stocking for Mabel too. Father Christmas is leaving her big gifts at home for when we return.

But I haven't got the faintest idea where Aunt Kate might have stashed the twins' stockings. There weren't any in the boxes of ornaments we found.

I can't even give him a pair of my socks. They don't go past my ankles.

'I'll just get them for you. Be right back!'

'You can leave them in Prunella's room. Thank you.'

Upstairs, I tear through all of Aunt Kate's drawers, but there's not even a leftover sock of Ivan's, let alone any Christmas stockings.

So, I don't really have much choice.

'Danny?' I call sweetly into the parlour. 'Can I see you out here for a minute, please?'

Danny and I throw ourselves onto the matching sofas, exhausted, after everyone has gone to their rooms and Mabel is finally in bed. She was thrilled that the twins turned their noses up at the peanut butter and jam sandwiches. It meant she got to gorge on them. The poor thing is probably upstairs now on a sugar high, trying to fall asleep so that Father Christmas can come.

Music drifts quietly from the record player in the corner. Aunt Kate's collection of classical music and opera fill one whole shelf, giving us all the Callas, Carrera and Pavarotti we could want.

'That went okay, considering,' Danny says, rubbing his bare legs. He'll have a cold drive home without his socks.

'It could hardly have gone worse! It's probably wrong to hate children, right?'

'Not those children,' he says. 'They deserve a slap. Along with their parents.'

'You did very well with them, though. You've got a knack with kids.'

'It helps to have your own.'

'You miss her.'

He nods. 'I think about her all the time. I'd move to America if I could, but that's not realistic. Without a way to work there legally, it would be a precarious way to live. I want to be a more stable influence in Phoebe's life, not a less stable one. It's got to stay like this for a while, but now that she's getting older, she'll soon get to stay with me during her holidays.'

The joy in his face makes me grin too.

'What about Mabel's father?' he asks. 'Is he in the picture?'

'No, he erased himself when I fell pregnant.' I give him the short answer. After all, I've known him for less than forty-eight hours, even if it feels a lot longer than that.

'We've been okay though, Mabel and I. We had my parents until three years ago, and Celine.'

'Ah, the mythical Celine you keep mentioning. She does sound incredible.'

'She is. She's part of our family.'

He watches me from beneath his mop of hair. 'You say that, but can anyone you're paying really be part of the family? At the end of the day, she is your employee, no matter how you feel about her. If something went really wrong then you could fire her. You can't do that with family. You're stuck with them through thick and thin, whether or not you want to be.'

'I'm sure it started out as a financial arrangement with my parents, but she's been with us since I was small, so she is part of my family.'

'Even though you pay her to cook and clean for you so you don't have to do it.'

I don't like his tone one bit. 'Don't make me sound like some spoilt silly rich woman. If you must know, we actually have very little extra money. Celine lives rent-free and we pay her a stipend.'

But that doesn't make it sound any better. What I mean is that, because she's part of the family, we all take care of each other.

Why am I being so defensive anyway? It doesn't matter what Danny thinks of us.

'You can go home now,' I say, pushing the discomfort from my mind. 'Can you be back by eight for breakfast?'

'You're the boss.'

'I didn't mean—'

'Good night, Lottie.'

He crosses the room in just a few seconds, until he's towering over me.

'Happy Christmas.' He leans down and kisses my cheek, and I feel the warmth of his lips long after he's left for home.

CHAPTER TEN

Sleep doesn't come easily, and it's not because I'm waiting for Father Christmas. I've got visions of Danny dancing in my head. Something about his vulnerability when he talks about his daughter tugs at my heart in a way it hasn't been tugged in years. So, it's really quite a shame that he thinks I'm a self-centred Londoner who exploits my "help".

And even if it has started to seem like we're just two friends together in this charade, I've got to remember that he's drawing a salary to be here.

It's just past six a.m. when I finally get up. Sleeplessness has won. Mabel stirs when I crawl out from under the duvet. I freeze. There's no way she'll go back to sleep this morning, not with a stocking full of presents waiting for her at the foot of our bed.

But she swallows in her sleep and turns over with a sigh. I don't risk kissing her.

'I love you, Mabel,' I whisper instead.

When I see the black shoes in the hallway, I have to laugh. Rupert has taken me up on my offer to polish them.

But my smile turns to a frown as I bend to pick them up. Oh no. Please say he hasn't. Tentatively I give them a sniff.

He has. Mingus has weed in Rupert's lace-ups.

That bloody cat!

How am I supposed to clean cat wee out of leather shoes? Even Martha Stewart would struggle with this one.

Rupert won't get into the Christmas spirit if he has to squelch around in wet shoes, so I can't wash them. But I've got to get that smell out somehow, because there's nothing festive about urine, either.

There must be something in the basement that might help. Bleach? No, can't get them wet. Soap powder could help soak up the wee, at least. But would that leave a white residue? He'll think I've been doing lines on his insoles. And if his feet get sweaty, he might end up with bubbles in his shoes.

Finally, I spot a bottle of Febreeze on the shelf above the washer. Ah, the miracle spray. I soak up as much of Mingus as possible with a cloth before giving each one a good blast.

I take them into the kitchen and give them the polish he wanted in the first place.

Now they smell of shoe polish and air freshener. He's definitely going to be suspicious of that.

Mingus rubs against my leg, purring like he hasn't just urinated in our guest's brogues.

'Bad cat!'

He looks perfectly innocent. 'Oh, I suppose now you think I ought to feed you? For that little stunt, you're getting chicken for breakfast.'

He sniffs at the dish and turns away.

As I'm putting the rest of his food packets away, I see Aunt Kate's spice cabinet. Which makes me wonder...

When I put Rupert's shoes back in front of his door, they smell deliciously of cloves, and faintly of shoe polish. He'll waft Christmas cake with every step today. Happy Christmas, Rupert.

I creep back to Aunt Kate's room to see if Mabel is awake.

'Good morning, Mummy,' she says when I open the door. She has her stocking clasped to her chest.

'Happy Christmas, Mabel! I see Father Christmas was here.'

'You didn't wake up either when he came in?'

Solemnly, I shake my head. 'I didn't see him.'

'I wonder how he always sneaks past us? He must be very quiet.'

'Would you like to open your presents? Remember, the ones from me are at home, and I bet Father Christmas left the big presents there too, so that we don't have to carry them back on the train.'

'He's very considerate. Is Danny awake yet?'

'He doesn't sleep here, honey. He has his own house, remember?'

'But he could sleep here if he wanted to, right? That would be all right with you, wouldn't it?'

What is she asking? 'You like Danny?'

'Oh, he is a good egg. I like him very much… do you like him, Mummy?'

'Well, yes, he seems like a nice bloke. And he's helping us a lot, isn't he?'

'Oh Mummy.' She rolls her eyes. 'I don't mean do you like him. I mean do you *like* him. Because he likes you.'

'What makes you say that?'

'Because he told me,' she says as a small green parcel at the top of the stocking grabs her attention. 'Should I open this one first?'

As much as I'm dying to ask her what Danny has said, it's not right to pump my seven-year-old for information.

I don't know when the twins will get to open their gifts, so we make a pact to keep our morning stocking raid a secret until later. Hopefully that way we'll avoid a double tantrum in case they're made to wait until after lunch.

'I'll just go have a quick bath while everyone is still asleep, okay?' I tell Mabel. 'Danny'll be here soon to fix breakfast.'

'Okay, Mummy, I'll go find Mingus. I think he might like to play with this.'

Out of all the gifts I've picked out over the past six months – gifts I was really excited about, like the silver charm bracelet and wild animal stencil art box and LEGO Architecture Big Ben – it's the pencil with googly eyes and blue feather hair that she loves most.

Next year Father Christmas is shopping at

Poundland.

'Mingus should have a Christmas too,' she continues, bouncing off the bed.

Mingus should have a kick in the backside.

I creep to the bathroom. Every extra minute that Rupert's family stays behind closed doors is precious. I don't know how Aunt Kate does this for a living. I wouldn't want to live around strangers all the time.

Flushing the loo, I go to wash my hands.

That's when I hear a weird rattling in the floor.

Oh no. I forgot to wait the five minutes after flushing that Cook warned us about.

Turning slowly, I see the grate over the drain cover in the middle of the tile floor start to vibrate.

Grrrrrrrrrrr, grrrrrrrrrrr, grrrrrrrrrrr... burp!

The grate lifts at one end, releasing a big turd that shoots across the floor, skidding to a stop next to the claw foot of the tub.

Probably not my turd, incidentally.

Water starts bubbling up behind it, covering the floor with a selection of our guests' leavings.

Oh, that is disgusting, and I speak as a mother who's dealt with more than her fair share of bowel movements that weren't hers. We'll have to bolt those drain covers to the floors.

Scooping the offending waste into the toilet, I mentally draft the polite wording to make little signs above each sink. I can just imagine Prunella's reaction if this had happened to her. Though, since nobody complained yesterday, it does mean that the guests must not be washing their hands. Delightful.

Danny is in the kitchen when I come down after my bath.

'Happy Christmas!' he says. He's wearing green and grey striped socks with his breeches.

'You're looking very festive.'

'Yeah, well these were the only other knee-length socks I've got.'

'I'm sorry I gave your others away.'

'No worries. I can buy a new pair with the £1,000 you're paying me.'

The mention of money makes me feel uncomfortable.

Stop it, Lottie. It's just a financial transaction. There's nothing to feel awkward about. Even if I am starting to wish that money wasn't part of the equation.

'Look what the ladies left for us.' He lifts the edge of the tea towel covering an assortment of oddly shaped eggs. No two are the same.

'That's scrambled eggs for everyone then.'

'And kippers. What else is on the menu today?' he asks.

I can't tell if he's also ill-at-ease about last night. Maybe he just thought he was making friendly conversation when he basically accused me of using Celine as cheap labour. Maybe he didn't get offended when I dismissed him and told him to come back today to work for us. Either way, he's looking at this as a financial arrangement to get him to Texas to see his daughter. I'm his boss for a few days, nothing more.

So, I guess that's the way I'd better start thinking

of it too. 'There's that beautiful beef in the fridge,' I say, trying to push any silly ideas about romance from my mind. 'I thought we could do that with potatoes and vegetables. And we've got the Christmas pudding for dessert. If we feed them enough, we may not have to make peanut butter sandwiches again tonight. Should we make lunch a little later, say, around four?'

'As long as the children won't have to wait until afterwards to open their presents. I used to hate having to wait.'

But we don't need to fear for the twins' feelings. I can hear them both screaming blue murder as they run down the stairs. Of course, Prunella and Hugo didn't make them wait. Those children get anything they want.

Rupert comes downstairs after his niece and nephew.

'Happy Christmas, did you sleep well?' Danny asks.

'Until the banshees woke, yes, thanks. Happy Christmas to you both. Is breakfast on the schedule this morning?'

'Absolutely!' I say. 'If you'd like to go in to the dining room, the table is set, so sit anywhere you'd like. I can bring in coffee or tea?'

'Coffee, please.'

'And would you like eggs? Beans? Kippers? Bacon and toast?'

'Yes, I'll have two soft-boiled eggs please.'

Somehow, I just knew he'd say that. Good luck to Danny finding two the same size.

Hugo and Prunella come into the dining room together, just as I'm serving Rupert his breakfast. It seems to be the one meal that Danny does actually know how to cook. Maybe we can convince our guests that the Victorians ate only fry-ups.

I'm not sure why I'm surprised that Hugo and Prunella have come down together. After all, they are married to each other. Whether they like it or not, their paths must cross sometimes – like two weather systems crashing into each other to make a miserable low-pressure system that washes out your Bank Holiday weekend.

'Beautiful day!' Hugo says, peering out the window at the bright blue sky. 'What's on the agenda before lunch?'

He looks at me.

Rupert looks at me.

Even Prunella deigns to look at me.

I guess it's my job to entertain them too. 'I'm afraid I'm not really from around here, so...'

'There are a few nice walking paths that run close to the house,' Danny says as he brings in a big pot of tea. He looks perfectly comfortable in the house now, like he lives here all the time. 'If you wanted to go for a walk after breakfast, I'll be happy to take you. It is a beautiful day. Lottie, would you like to come too?'

'Yes, Lottie, please do,' says Hugo.

And have Hugo try to drag me into the bushes? 'Oh no, thanks, you go ahead. I'll need to do some cleaning before lunch. Do take Mabel though, Danny, if you don't mind looking after her.'

'I don't mind at all. What do you say, Mabel? Do you want to come for a walk with us?'

She's just come into the dining room with Amanda and Oscar. All three are whispering together.

'Yes please!' Mabel says.

'What about you two?' Rupert asks. 'Do you fancy a little walk after breakfast?'

'I hate walks!' Amanda shouts. 'I won't go, and you can't make me.'

'Walks are for losers,' Oscar adds, looking straight at his uncle. 'That makes you a loser.'

I bet Rupert is really sorry not to have sprung for that holiday to Tanzania.

'Well then, you'll just have to stay here,' Prunella says. 'A walk will do me good. What time will we eat?'

'I'll just prepare everything before we go and we can eat around four,' Danny says.

'Make it two o'clock,' she demands. 'I don't want to eat late.'

CHAPTER ELEVEN

What have I gotten myself into? I'm used to parenting a moderately challenging but basically well-behaved child, not the spawn of Satan. I can't reason with Oscar and Amanda, and if I lock them in their room, they'll probably chew their way out.

'Well, I'm sure you got some nice presents from Father Christmas.' Although they deserve a lump of coal. 'Why don't you play with those?'

'I'm bored!'

'Me too.'

'Great, then you can come upstairs with me and clean the bathrooms. Shall I get you some rubber gloves?'

They run together into the parlour.

Sometimes reverse psychology does work.

I go into Prunella's room first. It's a tip. There are towels strewn all over the bed and the duvet has been pulled on to the floor. I wonder if that's where she makes Hugo sleep, in a little nest at the foot of the bed.

One end of the rug is covered in talcum powder and there are ring marks on the side tables where they haven't bothered to use the coasters. It's probably good that they usually go away for expensive holidays. At least then the hotel owners can use some of the money to fix what they've ruined during their stay.

I tidy up as best as I can, take a deep breath and move on to Rupert's room. Lord only knows what I'll find there.

But it doesn't even look like he's staying in the room. The bed is perfectly made. There isn't one personal item in sight. Does he levitate over the mattress, or sleep in the wardrobe, perhaps hanging upside down from the clothes rail?

The only clue that he's been there is that the bed is much neater than I managed to make it yesterday. Hats off to Rupert. He wins my vote for guest of the year.

The duvets are also pulled over the mattresses in the twins' room.

They may have the manners of the girls at St Trinian's, but at least the twins tried to make their beds, as slapdash as it is.

Smiling to myself, I whip back the first duvet to straighten it.

I smell bed-wetters.

This is literally a cover-up.

Mabel went through a short phase after my parents died, where nightly accidents became an issue, but, luckily, she stopped as suddenly as she started, and we haven't had to worry about it since.

I should be furious about Aunt Kate's wee-stained mattresses, but my heart goes out to the twins. They didn't do it on purpose.

Unlike the cat.

I find their sodden pyjamas balled up under one of the beds. I can wash and dry them and get them back to their room in time for bed. But the mattresses need cleaning.

After a lot of scrubbing, I'm just drying the second mattress with my hairdryer when I hear everyone coming back. They sound like they're in high spirits.

'Did you all have a good time?' I ask, watching Danny's expression for signs of a struggle.

'It was very nice,' he says. 'Look what Mabel found.'

She holds out a long feather. 'It's a peasant feather!'

'It's beautiful,' I say. 'I think you mean pheasant.'

She looks at Danny for confirmation. 'Pheasant,' she says. 'And we saw a live one too in the field.'

'I'm glad you had fun, but I'm glad you're back too. I missed you.' I hug her close.

'I'll just put lunch on,' Danny says.

'And how about some of that cocktail too?' Hugo asks. 'After all, it is a holiday, and nearly past noon. How were the children?'

'Oh, they were fine. I hardly even noticed them here,' I say.

'Where are they?'

I look around. That's a good question.

'They're off playing,' I say. 'Would you like a cup of tea to warm up? The parlour is toasty with the fire going.'

Once I get the adults safely into the parlour, I go looking for the children that I seem to have misplaced.

'Oscar, Amanda!' I whisper.

I check upstairs, behind all the curtains and under the beds.

'Are you playing hide and seek?'

I look in each cabinet and closet.

'Where are you, you little brats?!'

I get back downstairs to the kitchen just in time to see Danny cutting up the last bit of beef.

'What are you doing?!'

There's a huge mound of cubed beef on the chopping board.

'Just getting the meat ready for the stew. What are you doing?'

'I'm trying to find those flippin' children. Do you realise you've just cut up a Chateaubriand?'

'Are you speaking English?'

'It's supposed to be cooked whole and sliced at the table for everyone. Not used for stewing beef.'

That meat cost me nearly sixty quid. I glare at him. 'You don't really know how to cook, do you?'

'I thought that would have been obvious from yesterday.'

'Then why accept a job cooking?' I say, flinging open each of the cabinets, just in case there's a child wedged in there.

'You know why,' he mutters. 'And you would have

done exactly the same thing.'

He's right. Of course he's right. If Mabel lived on the other side of the world, I'd do anything to see her.

'I'm sorry,' I say. 'It's not like I could cook any of these ingredients either. I've just eaten out at nice restaurants in London, so I thought a few fancy meals would impress Rupert. I am really sorry.'

Suddenly it's really important for him to say that it's okay, that he forgives me.

'Lottie, I live on fry-ups and takeaways. If it's not Chinese, Indian or fish and chips, I haven't had much experience with it. So, I'm sorry. I should have told you I couldn't really cook.'

'Do you really know how to make a stew, or was this another salmon-in-salmon Danny special?'

He flinches. 'I think Mum used to put a bunch of meat and veg into a pot of water and boil it for a few hours. That should work, right?'

'Like I would know! While I go look for the twins, see if you can get a recipe off the internet.'

The twins aren't in the fridge either.

I'm starting to panic.

When I get back to the parlour, everyone is in the same position as yesterday. How quickly we find our routines, even when we're away.

'It is a lovely day,' I say, walking to each of the windows and pulling back the curtains.

No twins fall out.

'Would anyone like another board game? We've got lots here.'

I fling open the cabinet at the side of the

bookshelves. No children.

'Hugo, see if the twins are hungry,' says Prunella. 'If they are, the cook can make them lunch early.'

Hugo rises, draining his glass. 'Lottie, are the twins in the conservatory?'

'Um, they must be.'

I hurry after him.

Of course, they'll be in the conservatory. It's the sunniest room in the house and it's probably where Mingus is trying to snatch some peace and quiet. Besides, it seems to be his life goal to leave his fur on all the soft furnishings. He wouldn't want to miss out the sofas there.

I'm right about Mingus, at least. He's curled up on the back of one of the sofas.

'Hmm, where are they?' Hugh says. 'Lottie?'

I look all around, as if he's overlooked his own children.

'I'm afraid I don't exactly know.'

His eyes widen. 'You don't know? You don't know where my children are? They could be anywhere in the house?' His voice rises. 'Anywhere in the wood, for that matter? Or playing beside the road? Prunella!' he bellows.

Rupert marches into the conservatory a minute later. 'Must you shout, Hugo? What is it?'

'She's lost the children.'

Rupert looks confused. 'Lost them?'

'I haven't exactly lost them, Rupert. I just don't have them to hand right this second. I think they're hiding. They've got to be here somewhere, right?'

That sends them both off shouting for Oscar and Amanda. They stomp through all the rooms I've just looked in. By the time we all get back to the parlour, I'm nearly as panicked as they are.

But Prunella hasn't left the sofa. 'They must be here somewhere, Hugo. You know how they like to hide.'

'Prunella, you're worse than a cat when it comes to those children. Could you please at least try to care that they're missing? God, they might have been snatched. Were all the doors locked?' he asks me.

'I... I don't—'

Mabel has been watching this exchange with interest.

'They're probably in the dungeon,' she says.

'What dungeon, sugarpea?'

'Downstairs. I don't like it down there. I saw a spider.'

Her words send us all scrambling for the back stairs. We can hear the twins as soon as I open the door.

'Where's the light?' Hugo asks. 'I'm coming, darlings, I'm coming!'

Amanda and Oscar rush through the coal cellar door as soon as I open it. Their faces are black with ancient coal dust, except for teary streaks down their cheeks.

'We got locked in!' Amanda says, hugging her dad.

'It's pitch black in there, and cold,' adds Oscar. 'I thought the cat might be hiding in there.'

Rupert flicks the old-fashioned iron door latch up and down. 'You really should padlock this,' he says. 'It latches shut whenever the door is pulled closed.'

'I'm so sorry. I didn't think the children would go in there. I'll have Danny put a lock on it so it doesn't happen again. Oscar, Amanda, why don't we go upstairs by the fire so you can warm up? I'll draw your baths.'

The idea of bathing is clearly more upsetting than being locked in the coal cellar. Amanda's lip quivers.

'If you give me their clothes when they've changed,' I say to Hugo, 'I'll wash and dry them for you. Again, I really am sorry.'

I can feel Aunt Kate's rating slipping further from my grasp.

CHAPTER TWELVE

'The important thing is that you found them, Mummy,' Mabel says, snuggling closer on our bed. 'So, you shouldn't be upset any more. There was no harm done.'

If only that were true. What reviewer in his right mind is going to award a good rating to a B&B that's locked his relatives in the coal cellar? Even if they are monsters. He'll have to fail us on health and safety grounds alone.

Once we got the twins into their baths, I needed a few minutes to myself. I had just enough time for a minor breakdown before lunch.

Unfortunately, Mabel caught me in the act.

I don't like her to see me upset. When Mum and Dad died, I didn't have much choice. I was constantly in floods of tears. Now, if it's not a matter of life or death, I try really hard not to cry.

This might not be life or death, but it is Aunt

Kate's livelihood.

'Everything will be fine, I'm sure.' I sniff and straighten my dress. 'Shall we go downstairs and see if we can help Danny?'

'All right, but first I want to tell you something.'

'What is it?'

'I'm proud of you, Mummy. You've done your best and that's all we can ask of anyone. If you've done your best then you should hold your head up high.'

How many times have I said that to my darling girl? It's so nice to have some good words thrown back at me for a change.

'Thank you. I'm proud of us all. Remember what the house looked like when we first got here? Now look at it. Aunt Kate will be proud of us too. We'll serve Rupert and his family their Christmas dinner and see them on their way tomorrow.'

'I'll be glad to see the back of them,' she says. 'They're eating us out of house and home.'

That's Celine's favourite expression. At least I'm not the only one on Mabel's greatest hits list.

I send my daughter into the kitchen to see how Danny is getting on while I set the table for lunch. With a few pine boughs woven between the candles and the sparkling glasses and silverware, it looks quite festive by the time I'm finished. All I need are the Christmas crackers.

There are about a hundred in the cabinet under the stairs in the hall, but I have to crawl in to get them.

'Do you need a hand?'

Hugo is standing behind me, making me very aware that my head is in the cabinet and my arse is in the hall.

'No, I'm fine, thanks.'

'You look fine from here.'

I back out, shuffling the boxes of crackers as I go. 'How are Amanda and Oscar? Happy again?'

Maybe reminding him that he's fathered two children with Prunella will knock him off his game.

'There's no long-term damage. Here, let me help you with those.' He takes the boxes from me.

Fine, whatever. 'Thanks. I'll just set the table and then we're nearly ready for...'

He stops in the middle of the hall.

'Is something wrong?' I ask.

I stop too.

He shifts the boxes to one hand and points at the ceiling. 'Happy Christmas,' he says.

You have got to be kidding me. We're standing under the mistletoe that Danny hung to add a festive finishing touch for our guests' first impression. Clearly, it's making an impression on Hugo.

'I have to finish laying the table,' I say primly. 'I'll take those, thank you.'

I'll get Danny to take that flippin' mistletoe down too. I'd snatch it from the ceiling myself if I could reach. I'm definitely not asking Hugh for a boost up.

The beef stew actually smells delicious. It might not win

Danny any culinary awards for presentation, and it probably hasn't got the biggest wow-factor for Christmas lunch, but at least we're able to feed our guests.

They've downed an entire pitcher of cocktails by the time they pull their Christmas crackers, and here I am, I'm standing slumped against the fridge watching Danny microwave the Christmas pudding.

'Are you sure you're supposed to do that?' I ask him.

'There's not much choice now. It would need to steam for an hour and I forgot to start it before we served lunch. Besides, I looked it up on Google. The Google is never wrong.'

'My Mum never microwaved it.'

'That's because Celine did the cooking, right?'

'You don't have to be mean about it, you know.'

His eyebrows shoot up. 'I wasn't trying to be mean. Didn't Celine do the cooking? That's what you told me.'

'Mum also cooked.'

'Then I stand corrected. I'm sorry... why are you so sensitive when I mention Celine?'

'I'm not,' I say, sensitively. 'I just don't need anyone judging me, that's all.'

'Lottie. The last thing I'd ever do is judge you. Come on. You're a single mum who's had a horrible time. If anything, I'm jealous that you've got Celine. And I admire you.'

The blush creeps up my cheeks. He admires me!

'Thanks, Danny. You're pretty admirable yourself,

you know, the way you're devoted to your daughter. A lot of men don't bother.'

'I'm sorry about Mabel's father, Lottie, but not all men are tossers. I hope you do know that.'

'Well, I haven't run across very many since Mabel was born, tossers or otherwise, so I'll have to take your word on that.'

Danny is starting to restore my confidence though. If I were Phoebe's mother, I wouldn't have moved away.

The microwave pings and the moment passes.

I grab the brandy bottle and follow Danny to the dining room for our grand finale.

'Is everyone ready?' I say, holding the match over the booze-soaked pud. I always loved this part of Christmas lunch, when Dad would set our pudding alight, sending mum into a fit of sherry-soaked giggles. God, how I miss them.

I touch the match to the top of the pudding and it whooshes into blue flames that race down the sides.

Then the flames race around the plate.

Then they start racing across the linen tablecloth, following the trail of brandy I've managed to slosh there.

'Look, Mummy, it's like bonfire night,' says Amanda, remarkably calm for someone about to be caught in a house fire.

It takes only seconds for the flames to take hold.

'Get some water!' Hugo shouts, pulling his family away from the table.

I dash to the kitchen for a pot of water, but by the

time I get back, Danny is already there, pulling the pin on the fire extinguisher.

'I don't think we need—'

But it's too late. He aims the nozzle and shoots a white cloud of foam all over what's left of Christmas lunch.

The fire is out. As is any possibility of eating that pudding.

'We'll just go into the parlour,' Rupert says tactfully. 'Maybe we'll have our coffee in there?'

Looking at the bright side, at least we don't need to worry about keeping everyone out of the dining room when the 8.30 train passes tonight.

'I guess I overreacted,' Danny says, tucking his mobile phone away. He was talking to his daughter when I came upon him in the conservatory. I felt embarrassed catching him in such an intimate conversation, but his tone was so tender that I thought, once again, what a lucky little girl she is.

'Better safe than sorry, I guess. Aunt Kate wouldn't thank us if we burned her house down.'

He laughs. 'This has been the Fawlty Towers of Christmases. But it could have been worse.'

I raise my eyebrow. 'Please, tell me how that could be.'

'Well, at least we tried, and you can't do more than that.' He glances at my expression. 'Sorry, I was being a dad. It's just something I say to Phoebe.'

'I say the same thing to Mabel.'

For a moment we look at each other, possibly recognising our common bond as single parents. And maybe, I dare to hope, maybe just a little bit more.

'You'll want a ride over to the hospital,' he says. 'I'll drive you.'

And suddenly I'm back to being his employer again.

There's loads of activity around Aunt Kate's bed when we get to her room. Two nurses are there with Dr Lonergan. My heartbeat quickens. Something must be wrong. She's had a relapse. Or there's brain damage. Or worse. My eyes flick around the room, searching for those paddles they use to bring people back from the dead.

'Dr Lonergan, what's happening?'

When she smiles, relief washes over me. It's not bad news.

'We discontinued the medication and your aunt is coming around. We're just assessing her to make sure she's able to follow commands. Everything looks good.'

'Is she awake enough to know that we're here?'

'Why don't you ask her yourself?' she says, putting Aunt Kate's chart back into the slot at the end of her bed. 'We're finished now, so we can leave you in peace. Happy Christmas!'

It's probably completely inappropriate, but I pull her into a hug anyway. 'Thank you for everything you've done.'

'It's my pleasure,' she says, hugging me back. 'I

love a happy ending.'

Mabel and I bring the two grey plastic chairs close to Aunt Kate's bed. Maybe it's because she's sleeping instead of comatose, or because she no longer has the breathing mask over her face, or maybe it's my imagination now that I know the drugs have been stopped, but she looks different, better and more alive.

'Aunt Kate? It's Lottie.'

'And Mabel.'

'Today's Christmas Day, Aunt Kate, and the doctor says you're doing really well. That's the best present in the world for us. Things are still fine at the B&B. Everyone had a nice dinner.'

No need to mention that we almost had to ring the Fire Brigade.

'And Danny took everyone for a walk earlier. I think they're having a nice time.'

Best to keep the coal cellar incident quiet too.

'They'll leave tomorrow morning, so we can get back to normal and start looking forward to when you can come home.'

Though there's a bit of gloom on the horizon too. It's not just the reviewer who'll leave tomorrow, is it? Danny has stuck to our arrangement. Tomorrow he'll fulfil his promise and I'll have no reason to see him again.

'Can you hear me, Aunt Kate?'

'Her eyelids moved, Mummy! Did you see?'

'I did see!'

I feel my own eyes fill with tears. Aunt Kate really is coming back to us.

CHAPTER THIRTEEN

The guests are up early on Boxing Day, getting ready to escape back to London after breakfast. Danny's handiwork on the drains made sure there were no more smelly plumbing surprises, and I'm even starting to hope the guests might get away with no more mishaps.

The twins had one more go at destroying the parlour, pulling everything off the shelves before Hugo got them strapped into the car. They might end up being decent adults but, to quote Mabel quoting me, I'm definitely glad to see the back of them.

'So,' I say to Rupert as he hands me his room key. 'I do hope you enjoyed your stay with us. I'm sorry that there were a few... difficulties, but I hope that won't affect Aunt Kate's rating.'

He must know I'm being cheeky, but I've got nothing left to lose.

'It was an interesting visit,' he says. 'Please do

thank your aunt for inviting us. I'll be submitting my review in early January when I'm back from holiday.'

'Oh, are you going somewhere nice for New Year's?'

He nods. 'I'm flying to Tanzania tomorrow. On my own.'

I smile. 'I understand completely. It's not always easy having family around.'

'Some families are easier than others. Most families are easier than mine.'

That's true, though I'm probably not supposed to agree with him. 'So, the rating then... could you give me a hint about how it went?'

He peers over the pile of cases he's trying to wedge into the overfilled boot. 'Well, I wasn't fooled by your Victorian theme. It was pretty clear you were bluffing by the time the peanut butter sandwiches came out. But I liked that you carried on with it in the face of complete implausibility. You're clearly very good at handling difficult guests. Frankly, I'd have kicked Hugo in the bollocks and gone straight to my sister, so you showed remarkable restraint there.'

He wouldn't think so if he knew I'd bitten his brother-in-law.

'The food was interesting...' he continues.

'It didn't turn out quite like I'd imagined.'

'Locking the children in the coal cellar when you were meant to be minding them certainly wasn't clever.'

I can't do anything but nod. I feel like the worst innkeeper in Britain. Maybe there's a prize for that. I may as well win something.

'And I've never seen a host set their dining table on fire before.'

The twins *did* think that was pretty cool though, so we're due some points for entertainment, at least.

'But at the end of the day, I came here to assess the B&B, which your aunt owns and runs. Presumably she runs it better than you.'

Ouch.

'It's definitely not perfect,' he continues, 'and she needs to sort out her plumbing before the health inspectors shut her down. As a B&B, this is a reasonable business and does meet enough of our standards to warrant the rating.'

'Really?! That's wonderful, thank you so much!' I launch myself on Rupert.

'Ehem, yes, well, you're welcome.'

'Phew. I didn't think you were going to give it to us.'

The tiniest of smiles plays around his lips. 'Prunella doesn't like to admit it, but our Granny's house looked a lot like this. It was draughty and a bit run down, but the weekends I spent there as a child, lying in front of the fire in the parlour and eating Granny's cakes each teatime, are some of my happiest memories. Your aunt has a special place here.' He brushes himself off and clears his throat. 'And as I said, most of the faults were because of you, not the B&B per se... you're not thinking of staying on to run it, are you?'

I shake my head. 'No, I'll go back to software

programming where I belong.'

'That's best for everyone.'

Mabel, Danny and I wave them off just before noon.

'That's that then,' says Danny as they pull out of sight.

That *is* that, then. We've done what we set out to do. Unless I do something fast, Danny is going to drive away from Aunt Kate's B&B and out of my life. I've got no idea where things could lead with him, or even if he'd be interested in finding out. We might be completely ill-suited for each other, with nothing in common now that there'll be no B&B to run. What do I know is that I like Danny, and it's not for his cookery skills.

'I've been thinking about the decorations inside,' I say to him as Mabel runs back into the house to find Mingus. 'And I could use help taking some of them down. Only the ones that I need the ladder to reach. I'd like to leave all the others for when Aunt Kate comes home. I just don't want to climb up without someone holding the ladder, and, erm, with Aunt Kate's broken leg, I can't ask her for help later. Could you spare another half hour or so?'

I know I'm being ridiculous, playing the helpless female to draw out my time with him. My inner feminist is hanging her head in shame. But my heart is hoping a few more minutes might make some kind of difference.

'Of course,' he says, wrestling the ladder in from outside. He's not wasting any time. This was a stupid idea.

He sets it up against the first window in the hall. 'Do you want to climb up or hold the ladder?'

'I'd better climb,' I say. 'I'm not sure I could catch you if you fell off.'

'You've got a lot of faith in me.'

I pluck the pine boughs from the top of the valance and drop them on the floor. Well, at least this is one job I won't have to do next week. I always find it depressing to take down the decorations. 'We got the rating, you know.'

'You are joking!' he says. 'What were his criteria? Missing persons and pyrotechnics?'

I climb down and let him carry the ladder to the next window. Then I pull down more boughs, smiling as the pine scent washes over me. It will be nice to get Aunt Kate home where we can have Christmas together. I might even try to cook that stew for her.

'He said he appreciated our efforts,' I tell him. 'Though he didn't buy the Victorian theme.'

'That reminds me. I never did get my socks back.'

'Sorry about that. I noticed Hugo packing them in the car. It didn't seem like a good time to tell him his children's Christmas stockings had come straight off your feet.'

We move to the last window.

'They were such a weird family,' he says.

He doesn't know the half of it. 'Rupert is going to Tanzania tomorrow, on his own.'

'I don't blame him. I'd rather take my chances out in the bush with lions than spend any more time with

Prunella.'

The last of the boughs hits the floor. 'That's all of them.'

I climb down.

'What about the mistletoe?'

It hangs there in the middle of the hall, an unwanted reminder of Hugo's attentions.

Danny positions the ladder beneath it, and puts his hands on either side of me so that I can climb up.

'Lottie? Wait a minute. There's something I—'

As I turn to face him, his warm lips meet mine. They're so perfectly soft, but a little bit urgent, and I know I want to stay in exactly this position for a very long time.

'I'm sorry,' he says. 'I couldn't think of a better way to tell you. I'm very out of practice.' He kisses me again. 'I haven't felt like this about anyone in a long time. We make a good team.'

'Are we talking about the B&B?' I kiss him back.

'I hope we're talking about everything,' he murmurs as we break off our kiss. 'But we must have done something right here. To get the rating, I mean.'

I think we're doing a lot of things right and, at this very second, I couldn't care less about the rating. 'They must have just loved your food.'

'Very funny.'

'No really, it wasn't bad. Although I wouldn't bother buying you expensive ingredients again.'

'Next time you can cook your own food.'

'I think we both know that I can't do that.'

'Then for both our sakes, I think I'd better take

you out to dinner.'

We kiss again under the mistletoe.

Danny drives us to the hospital that afternoon as usual. But instead of sitting in the back seat, I sit up front so I can hold his hand between gear changes. Every time I look in the rear-view mirror, I catch Mabel's grin.

'We'll be two hours,' I tell Danny.

'Okay, I'll run home quickly, but I'll be here waiting when you get out.'

'Just like you were the first day.'

He smiles and kisses me again. 'Some things are worth waiting for.'

'Danny, there'll be plenty of time for that later,' Mabel says. 'Right now, we need to see Aunt Kate.'

I shrug. 'She's seven going on seventeen.'

'She's her mother's daughter. See you soon.'

'Aunt Kate, you're awake!' Mabel says when we get to her room. 'We've got so much to tell you!'

'Hello, love.' She pats the mattress beside her.

'Careful, Mabel,' I warn. 'How are you feeling?'

I take my aunt's hand.

'I feel like I've been run down by a lorry, but it's better than the alternative. I gather I've been sleeping for a while.'

'Five days. The doctor has been great.'

She nods. 'She must have thought there's some life left in these old bones yet.'

'Mummy has a boyfriend,' Mabel says.

Aunt Kate peers at me. 'Does she now?'

Mabel nods. 'His name is Danny and he's our cook but not really our cook. He's also our taxi driver. But not really that, either. He's really our friend. That's right, isn't it, Mummy?'

'That's right. There's a lot to tell you, Aunt Kate, but most importantly, the reviewer loved the B&B and he's going to give you the rating you need.'

'Oh, that is wonderful news! So, everything went well then?'

'Except for the fire,' says Mabel.

'Like I said, there's a lot to tell you. Are you tired, though? We can always talk more tomorrow if you want to rest.'

'Don't you dare leave, Lottie. I want to hear every detail. Especially about this boyfriend of yours.'

But I start with the B&B, since that's probably what Aunt Kate really wants to hear about. Mabel doesn't let me gloss over any of the gory details. She's a stickler for the whole truth, not to mention a very observant little girl who seemed to know that Danny and I liked each other before we'd realised it ourselves.

'I'm just sorry that I've missed Christmas,' Aunt Kate says. 'I do so love the holidays.'

'You haven't missed it. We're staying here until you get out, and then we'll all have Christmas together.'

'Will you really?'

I nod. 'I'm not going back to London just yet. You'll need help while your leg is healing, and I can work remotely for a few weeks. I'll have my computer couriered up. Mabel doesn't have to be back in school until mid-January.'

'That will be wonderful, Lottie,' Aunt Kate says. 'It's all worked out quite wonderfully, really.'

As promised, Danny is waiting for us when we leave the hospital.

'Aunt Kate's awake!' Mabel says. 'And we get to stay in Wales to have another Christmas. Does that mean we get more presents from Father Christmas, Mummy?'

'No, honey, I'm afraid he doesn't do encore performances. You'll have to wait till next year, but remember you've still got lots of gifts at home.'

'You are staying here for a while?' Danny asks, grabbing my hand.

'For a few weeks at least,' I say. 'Till Mabel needs to be back for school.'

'I fly to the US tomorrow, but I'll be back in a week.'

'And then…'

'And then we'll work something out,' he says. 'It's not ideal with me here and you in London, but it is only a few hours by train. I could come down and, if you don't mind travelling a bit, you and Mabel could come here too?'

We kiss again. I can't seem to get enough of him. 'I don't mind at all. What do you say, Mabel? Would you like to spend more weekends at Aunt Kate's?'

'Definitely, Mummy. Now that Mingus and I are friends, he'd be sad if we didn't see each other. And Aunt Kate still needs to make me her Welsh cakes. I could murder one of those.'

'I'll tell you what, Mabel,' says Danny. 'I'll look up

a recipe on the internet and make you some when we get back to the B&B. It'll be good practice.'

We both stare at him.

'That's okay, Danny,' Mabel says, patting his shoulder over the back of the driver's seat. 'No offense, but I can wait for Aunt Kate to make them. You'd better practice being Mummy's boyfriend. I think you'll be a lot better at that.'

The End

ABOUT THE AUTHOR

Lilly Bartlett is the pen-name of Sunday Times and USA Today best-selling author, Michele Gorman, who writes best friend-girl power comedies under her own name.

Michele writes books packed with heart and humour. Call them beach books, summer reads or chick lit... readers and reviewers call them "feel good", "relatable" and "thought-provoking".

Michele was raised in the US and now lives in London. She is very fond of naps, ice cream and Richard Curtis films but objects to spiders.

Printed in Great
Britain
by Amazon